Aphrodite

Aphrodite

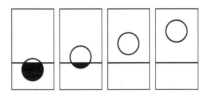

Yamada Masaki

Translated by
Daniel Jackson

KURODAHAN PRESS

Aphrodite

Copyright © 1980 Yamada Masaki
Originally published in Japan as *Afurodite* by Kōdansha, Tokyo
English translation copyright © 2004, 2019 Daniel Jackson
This edition © 2004, 2019 Kurodahan Press
All rights reserved.

Cover: Kobayashi Osamu

FG-JP0002-A3
ISBN-13 978-4-902075-01-4
ISBN-10 4-902075-01-6

KURODAHAN.COM

Contents

2018 :: Age 18	1
2023 :: Age 23	55
2028 :: Age 28	105
2063 :: Age 30	155
Author's note	205
About the Author	206
About the Translator	207
About the Artist	208

2018 :: Age 18

1

MORNING.

Yūichi woke up.

He automatically held his right hand over his face, trying to block the daylight seeping in through the cracks in the blinds. He mumbled something to himself. Behind his hand, he blinked his eyes two or three times. Finally he gave up and opened his eyes.

Yūichi lay for a while, looking at the ceiling.

He heard the sound of the waves . . . loud, soft, loud, soft. . . . Gradually, the sparkle of life returned to Yūichi's eyes. He rolled his eyeballs once. Slowly, he stretched his legs out straight, and tossed aside the blanket. He swung his legs out over the edge of the bed, like pendulums, and, without using his hands, sprang out of bed.

He came to a smooth landing on the floor, with a neat *thump*. He didn't lose his balance or falter: superb form, like a gymnast dismounting the parallel bars.

Planting his chin on his chest, and placing his arms flat against his sides, he stood where he was, still.

The sound of waves.

Suddenly, Yūichi's body became shorter . . . then taller . . . then shorter . . . as Yūichi repeated his deep knee bend exercises. Sometimes he twisted his upper torso with all his might. His waist was firm, his body bouncing like a spring.

After continuing the knee bends for about five minutes, Yūichi stood up straight, as if he wanted to stretch backwards. His bare chest was slightly moist with sweat. His breathing was not ragged. Yūichi lightly pinched his belly muscle, and smiled in triumph. The muscles were firm: plenty firm, and with plenty of tension.

They were the muscles of an eighteen-year-old. Yūichi strode across the room, and rolled the blinds all the way to the top with a single pull.

The sunlight came crashing into the room.

For one instant, his field of vision was painted over in pure white; then undulating greens and blues gradually opened up.

Sunlight, and sky, and the sea.

The sea came to life in the morning sun: waves were rolling in, and returning; the surf drummed in the distance.

A hydrofoil was cutting across the bay. Framed in a triangle of glittering radiance, it looked as if it were flying through the air.

Gulls spread out in the sky, slowly circling. Occasionally the sun flashed off a gull's wings into Yūichi's eyes.

Wow!

Yūichi felt a shout of joy rising from the core of his heart. However many times he saw it, he could never get used to the wonder of Aphrodite: the floating city. He felt fresh surprise every time, and shouted it out:

"Wow!"

Sweat came springing out on Yūichi's bare chest.

2018 :: Age 18

Even though it was morning, the sun of the southern seas was still strong. The air itself was already hot.

Even with the heat, though, nobody was so un-cool as to want weather control for Aphrodite. The air was very dry, so it was not an unpleasant heat.

If you didn't like the heat you could move to the North Pole easily enough, or to the South Pole, or *anywhere*. No one would stand in your way.

He liked the heat, and had never even thought of leaving. Quite the opposite: he wanted to live here the rest of his life.

Yūichi waved his hand slightly, saying goodbye to the sights outside his window, and walked to the bathroom. He took a cold shower, then rubbed himself pink with a fresh towel. Now, if not before, he was wide awake.

Yūichi dashed instant coffee into a pot of boiling water, and began to warm the frying pan. He dropped a few thick slices of ham and four eggs into the butter-smeared fry pan, poured in a touch of water, and set on the lid. He could hear the sound of sputtering grease, and a mouthwatering smell started to drift through the kitchen.

Yūichi grinned.

Today's going to be a good day, too, he felt. He knew it: no doubt about it, it was going to be a wonderful day....

▲

MAKITA YŪICHI HAD COME to Aphrodite, the floating city, one year before.

The reason, to put it simply, was that Yūichi loved the sea. And he hated Tokyo.

In Yūichi's opinion, Tokyo was no place for people to live. The ocean was filthy. The air was filthy. And, above all, there were too many people. He was suffocated by it all.

"You keep saying that kind of thing, you'll never make it in the world," his mother would say. "You'll never become a somebody."

"Looks like your future's already made."

His older brother had graduated with honors from one of the best universities. He used to say, scornfully, "You're going to be a drifter . . . nothing but. You can't even be a janitor. These days, there aren't any companies crazy enough to employ a janitor. A robot is so much cheaper. . . ."

From where he was now, it seemed that his father dying when Yūichi was thirteen years old was maybe a blessing after all. . . . His short-tempered father would have beaten him all the time.

Of course, Yūichi had talked back to his mother and brother, and they had shouting fights. Yūichi had fought hard. Unfortunately, to look at it objectively, he had to admit—as much as it hurt—that, after all, his mother and brother had been right.

It was true.

If he had continued that way, he certainly hadn't seemed likely to become a somebody. He had sensed the truth of his brother's prophecy: him becoming a drifter. It became a habit to look out for the drifters on the street, and observe them—fixate on them—wretchedly, for his own future reference. True, in that totally managed city, observing how the drifters ate, and how they tenaciously held on to life, was a kind of study and sometimes even deeply moving. He learned a lot; but as a career path for a sixteen

2018 :: Age 18

year-old, he had to admit it was a—no, a *very*—miserable choice.

That was not to say that Yūichi was a lazy good-for-nothing, and to say that he was a failure as a person didn't quite fit either. He had no—well, only no *major*—criminal tendencies.

In that case, what was it that had shaped him like a parent; that had destroyed his hopes for his own future?

The explanation was all in one word. Yūichi was a *romantic*.

He had been a boy of many dreams. He thought he wanted to create his own future, all by himself. He loved the sea more than anything else ... and that was all.

To a person trying to live in Tokyo, that in itself was a fatal handicap.

In Tokyo—officially the "Tokaido Megalopolis"—romantics were on the brink of extinction. The Society for the Preservation of Endangered Species took no interest in the disappearing romantic. In a few years time, it wouldn't be strange to see a romantic preserved in formalin in a science museum.

Japan was a culture of total competition.

Kick down, drag down, attack unawares ... that was the philosophy ruling the Japanese, and their morals. A trend already manifest at the end of the 20th century, later spurred along ever more strongly—ignoring and crushing out murmurs of *I want to live like a human being and relax*—avalanching unchanged into the 21st century. Put bait at the exit, release some mice into the cardboard maze ... that's what it was. Even knowing that only one of them would win the prize, the mice had no choice but to scurry. Because if they didn't scurry, they lost even the chance of being that one lucky mouse.

People scurried.

Gasping for breath, throttling and raking at their competitors' eyes as they went, they still scurried. They kept on going—all just to push up Japan's GNP.

A delightful way to be.

Unfortunately for him, though, Yūichi didn't want to scurry. No. He didn't mind running, but first he wanted to know that there was a reward at the end, and that it was a reward he wanted. Without that, even if he were dragged down, he didn't feel like trying to lead the pack.

That kind of person was what you called a *romantic*. And so, in Japan, a romantic was nothing more than another name for a useless person.

Yūichi felt totally put out.

He wrinkled his short nose, and lines appeared on his boyish forehead, as he thought that—maybe—he had been too simplistic after all.

Maybe it was arrogant to want to steer clear of the competition for the time being, working at part-time jobs until he found the job that he really wanted to do. Maybe it was nothing more than the foolish dream of a child who didn't know the real world. . . .

Maybe so. Then again, maybe not. . . . Yūichi just didn't know.

The people around him spurred him on incessantly—browbeat him, sometimes trying to coax him—to somehow open his eyes to the reality of their competition-based society. All of them said the same thing: "You're a lazy, worthless dog; just a coward hiding your eyes from reality." Yūichi

2018 :: Age 18

thought their evaluation was totally, terribly, beside the point. Why wouldn't people understand? Even Yūichi had the same desire to run. . . . But, where to run *to*? That was what he didn't know.

Yūichi grew angry, and his life, too, became wild.

Around that time, Yūichi saw an old, old movie—it was even older than 3D photos!—called "Rebel Without a Cause", and was deeply moved. In spite of his long legs and the difference in their looks he felt that the audacity and brazenness of James Dean's young man was just like himself.

Yūichi began to hang out on the street in a regent hairstyle and a black leather jacket. He amused himself with a slightly sad, sullen expression, even though other people thought he was only pouting.

The truth of it—what Yūichi thought to himself—was that he was just fated to drop out of competitive society. It seemed like his brother's prediction, of him becoming a drifter, would hit the mark, if he kept going the way he was.

That was because, in that spurred, ever-accelerating competitive society, it was not easy to be true to a *rebellion without a cause*.

Fortunately—he should be punished for his impenitence, but he really did think that way—his mother died suddenly of an illness.

Of course Yūichi was very sad, but at the same time he couldn't deny an inexpressible sense of liberation.

"I'll take the house and land, because I'm the eldest son," said his brother, firmly. "I'll give you a reasonably large sum of cash. Take it, and I don't want to see you again."

Truly, he had to agree it had been a reasonable offer. Yūichi didn't ever want to see his brother's face again, either. Yūichi took the money, and went straight to the office of an airline company.

He didn't really want to go anywhere in particular. As long as it was outside suffocating Japan, anywhere was fine. . . . And anyway, he wanted to live in a foreign country.

The very first thing that caught Yūichi's eye when he set foot in the travel company's office was a tourist poster for Aphrodite, the floating city.

It was nothing more than the usual sort of tourist poster you could see anywhere: a long shot of the sea-shell shaped Aphrodite rising up startlingly out of the radiance, against a background of blue ocean.

Yūichi had no particular interest in Aphrodite. Quite honestly, he didn't even know too accurately where it was.

But he ended up buying a ticket to Aphrodite. . . . He thought a city on the sea would not lock up the sea, and the price of the ticket was low enough for him to buy with what he had. Maybe the real reason was that deciding between some place here, or there, or over there, was just too much trouble.

When he thought about it later, he was forced to admit that the choice had been made out of despair.

At any rate, a few hours after walking into the office, Yūichi was on an HST bound for Aphrodite. Even then Yūichi had absolutely no idea what kind of place he was going to. It had been a month after his seventeenth birthday. . . .

▲

2018 :: Age 18

WHEN YŪICHI FINISHED HIS meal, he splashed soap and water over the plates, busied himself here and there, and stepped out in his swim trunks.

The strong sun hit him, and he had to close his eyes for a second. He felt as if the moisture in his skin puffed away, evaporated.

Hot.

He automatically wiped the sweat from his neck, rubbing his damp hand on his trunks, then bounded down the small path to the harbor. Reflected light flashed from the green leaves of the tropical trees flanking the road. The red of the hibiscus shone into his eyes... and when the wind blew, the rustling leaves whispered, and sparkles rippled like glass crystals, and the sweet aroma of sap spread lazily through the air.

Yūichi liked this road when he walked this way, the joy of having escaped that trashy Tokyo filling his heart. Compared to Aphrodite, Tokyo was like... was like... a cesspool! *It's true*, Yūichi nodded to himself. Tokyo is a toilet. A scrap heap, a junk yard. Even the people are rotting, the stench rising....

Yūichi came out to the walkway along the bay, stopped, and slowly turned and looked back. Again, he was seized with happiness.

From where he stood, it looked just like there was a huge hilly region running along the shoreline of the bay. It looked as though the thick tropical plants had been cleared here and there, and houses set into a step-like layout—but the reality was quite a bit different.

Aphrodite was a floating city, an artificial island. Here, natural hills and free-growing tropical plants were impossible. Every single thing—every tree, each blade of grass—had been brought into this world by human hands.

Of course, Yūichi knew that. He knew it, but when he looked at those houses on the hills, when he saw this area, called "Herleg", he couldn't help but feel the beauty of nature.

He couldn't hold back his admiration, his praise.

"*Wow!*"

He had to let it out in a shout.

Can you believe it?

Above Aphrodite towered an artificial mountain, called "Herhead." It rose only three hundred meters above sea level, but was covered with fresh green plants, with a single ridgeline running for two kilometers.

If more than half of the inhabitants wanted—it hadn't been put to the test yet—to move Aphrodite northward, they could turn it into a huge ski slope.

Encompassing the front of Aphrodite was a purple coral atoll. Even that atoll was actually a skillfully camouflaged wave-protection damper: a wave-damping device made of fifty-meter raft-like breakers linked together.

People might condemn it as a sham, but in spite of all preconceptions every person who saw Aphrodite—for example, Yūichi—was touched by its natural beauty.

Yūichi continued along the walkway.

This harbor, set in Herleg sector, was primarily used as a harbor for privately-owned boats. Walking along the bay, he could see yachts, big cruisers, hovercraft, water-scooters, and even rocket-propelled submersibles at their moorings, and he never grew tired of the sight. It was a special treat for a young man like Yūichi who loved the sea so much.

2018 :: Age 18

A supertanker was slowly crossing the bay.

Looking across the bay to the opposite shore, to Herhip sector, it was possible to see everything distinctly, even each individual house. Everything was outlined clearly under the bright sun, haze-free.

Yūichi felt like whistling.

His workplace—the boat harbor where the small submersible *Rosebud* was moored—came into view.

Rosebud was the private boat of Aphrodite's mayor, G. Caan, and Yūichi was employed as Mr. Caan's boat boy.

Whatever else you might say, you had to agree that Yūichi was a lucky young man. He loved this land of Aphrodite, and he had fallen head-over-heels in love with his workplace, the *Rosebud*.

And *Rosebud* was, indeed, a beautiful craft. A masterpiece of art and technology outstanding even here in Aphrodite.

The capabilities of submersibles had begun to advance rapidly after rocket engine propulsion became a reality. Rocket propulsion was high-energy, relatively low weight, and had the advantage of not needing air. It seemed almost made for propelling submersibles.

Thanks to the development of the rocket engine propulsion system, submersibles had become faster and their underwater endurance had been vastly extended. The only drawback was the high cost, but the manufacturers had somehow managed to bring that down to about the same level as a luxury yacht.

Even so, they were well out of the reach of the average person. Even on Aphrodite, there were probably fewer than a hundred people who owned a rocket engine submersible.

Yūichi stuck his hands on his hips, stood on the pier, and stared lovingly at the *Rosebud*.

Over half a year had passed since he had been employed by Mr. Caan, but he still had to stop and drink in the beauty of the *Rosebud*. It was a ritual to him, as he might do for a girl he fell in love with.

Rosebud was a two-seater, and looked like a cigar-shaped cylinder. Its actual structure was more of a linked series of spheres, but you wouldn't guess that from the outside. It was designed very simply; and, of course, the main engine opening was below the water line, where it couldn't be seen.

Overall, *Rosebud's* curved lines were elegance itself, and although a novice might think she was just an uncouth and clumsy diving saucer, the truth was different. The speed of a diving saucer was just slightly over five knots, while the *Rosebud* could easily do submersible-class twenty knots—probably twenty-five knots with the rocket engine full open. Submersibles were used quite differently from the military subs. Fitted with lights and manipulators, they could dive slightly deeper than submarines, and they were often used for various types of submerged work. Compared to the typical submersible, the *Rosebud's* twenty to twenty-five knot speed was truly exceptional.

The tiny rosebud painted on the stern was what gave the *Rosebud* that special chic and allure. Every time he saw it, his chest grew tight with longing.

Yūichi, who had been drifting aimlessly through life like a rudderless ship, began to settle down after coming here, and focus on a single future.

He wanted to somehow make submersibles his life's work. He hadn't thought concretely yet about what form that work might take, but he had decided in his heart to work with them the rest of his life.

He was stunned to see what a difference it made to have a goal in life. Everything he did had a spring in it; he felt as if . . . *as if his heart were in it now.* It was a big difference from hanging around and pouting on the bustling streets of Tokyo.

Yūichi himself had become almost charming, compared to what he had been when he had wanted to be like James Dean. He started to laugh a lot. Fundamentally, Yūichi was an optimistic young man who didn't much care for formalities.

The fact that his heart was in his work may have been because Yūichi worked for the most powerful man in Aphrodite—Mr. Caan—so he might get citizenship quicker than he could in other jobs. If he had citizenship, it would be easy to get a submersible license. As a boat boy, of course, it went without saying that he could get practice piloting a submersible. . . . Everything was planned with an eye to the future. His heart was in it.

Yūichi let out a sigh, and at last tore himself away from the boat's beauty. Today, he had to wash the interior of *Rosebud's* fuel tank. It wasn't his job to stand here all day, staring at the boat he had fallen in love with.

Yūichi, smiling sourly, turned his head and walked toward the *Rosebud*. As he placed one foot on the deck, a voice from behind stopped him.

▲▲▲▲ 2

"IF YOU'RE GOING TO wash the tank, tomorrow's just as good," said the voice.

Yūichi turned, and his face brightened. He said happily, "Good morning, sir."

Yūichi's employer, Mr. Caan, was standing on the dock.

Mr. Caan was fifty-four years old, with whitening hair, but a youthful face and a sun-tanned body with little fat. He had the physique of a man in his thirties.

Twenty years ago, when Aphrodite was still being advanced as a United Nations city, Mr. Caan had been a member of the planning committee.

By then he was already a top-notch architect, known throughout the world as a city-engineering specialist. He was also famous as a sportsman and international playboy.

Mr. Caan led a bright life; he was a star. A mover and a shaker, he had been welcomed as a member of the planning committee. They said that he poured all of his city-engineering knowledge and personal architectural skill into the project, striving to create an attainable utopia.

Just as a child might be taken by a toy, so Mr. Caan was taken by the building of Aphrodite. Of course, he was not a child. He was a first-class architect, a city-planning specialist, a sportsman, an international playboy, and, in addition, a wielder of vast political power.

In a sense, you could say he was a utopian visionary. At the same time, he was a vital, ambitious man.

After he joined the committee, the blueprints underwent vast changes. First of all, the planned United Nations building, heliport, hotel/underwater restaurant complex and oceanographic research institute became a town, and the scale of Aphrodite, too, changed. At some point, the construction plans for Aphrodite began to ignore its character as a UN facility, and began to develop as an entirely new city.

Of course, not all the other committee members concurred with Mr. Caan's lone-wolf designs. Some voiced strong dissent, others got angry or left the committee entirely, but on the whole the other members observed his single-handed efforts silently, smiling—because it was clear that his designs were on a scale far larger than the UN's plans. The fact was, they thought it was only an unrealizable plan: A utopian dreamer, they said to each other, sharing a common judgment.

When the ocean city project was later transferred from the control of the UN to the major economic powers, primarily America, and they realized they would be expelled from the committee, they were furious. Mr. Caan earned quite a reputation as a behind-the-scenes manipulator.

He met with various heads of state, and somehow succeeded in raising enough capital for the construction of Aphrodite. The success was entirely due to the struggle of a single man: it became the source of countless stories, a legend in this world of totally managed societies.

2018 :: Age 18

Mr. Caan succeeded in winning funding from the industrialized West because Aphrodite promised full return for the money invested. There would always be many oil-drilling ships on stand-by at Aphrodite. The city itself could not be used as a drilling platform, but as a base for drilling ships, even for tankers, Aphrodite could be used in any way at all. Furthermore, when sea-bottom oil deposits were discovered—depending on the estimated need—Aphrodite would move closer to the site, and provide all the necessary assistance and labor.

It is easy to imagine how attractive that proposal was to the oil companies. It was impossible to know where a good oil field might be discovered, but now, whenever and wherever, skilled labor would be available.

Aphrodite's contribution to undersea mining exploration was not limited to petroleum. Coal, natural gas, the gold sand of Alaska, Southwest African diamonds, Indonesian tin—the list went on and on. The potential value of Aphrodite was immeasurable.

Mr. Caan had firmly refused to allow Aphrodite to be used as a drilling platform. Aphrodite would supply skilled labor, but a drilling platform always revealed its function in its exterior design. By repeated argument, Mr. Caan was able to protect the character of the new city's suburban dwellings, the business sector, the plaza, the recreation area—for Mr. Caan, changing Aphrodite to a land of noise and smoke was flatly unacceptable. He himself said that if that were the only option, it would be better not to build it at all.

At last, his opinions were accepted, and Aphrodite began to be built, with the goal of creating clean new streets and land.

America, England, Germany, France—all backed the project completely, supplying capital and human resources. Aphrodite's administration, by cooperating with their national energy policies, managed to protect its status as a sort of vaguely independent nation, rather than a colony of any one power.

Aphrodite accepted immigrants from many countries, from artists to refugees: it accepted them all gladly. Mr. Caan's plan seemed to be to make Aphrodite into a crucible for humanity, a sort of multi-ethnic kingdom.

He cut off immigration when the number of people seeking permanent residence passed two hundred thousand. He reasoned that if the population exceeded that limit, the city's functions would begin to suffer from "hardening of the arteries." He believed that a population of two hundred thousand was most suitable for the composition of a city, in every meaning.

Aphrodite was a modern fairy tale, and Mr. Caan had just turned forty when that fairy tale became a reality.

In the past, as in the present, the people who hated Mr. Caan were legion. Fortunately, however, far more people liked him, and Yūichi was one. Whenever he met Mr. Caan, he became happy for no clear reason. His voice always revealed his happiness.

"Morning." Mr. Caan returned Yūichi's greeting. "Wash the fuel tank tomorrow. Sorry, but would you run my wife over to the airport?"

"Your wife, sir?

"Uh huh."

Mr. Caan nodded, and gave a short laugh. "It

2018 :: Age 18

would be better if I could take her, but I got my license suspended last night for a speeding violation."

Yūichi couldn't help laughing.

Mr. Caan's speed madness was widely known. It was said that the reason he hadn't made all the roads electronically controlled highways was that he was afraid of having his own driving pleasure stolen from him. His fans loved it as an expression of his spirit of adventure, while his enemies condemned it as the worst kind of authoritarian egoism.

In any case, Mr. Caan insisted on driving his own EV. And so, the ritual of license lifting and license re-issuing was repeated and repeated.

"Making her go by auto-bus, there's just too much baggage," he said. "If you take her to the airport, you can have the rest of the day off."

"Right, sir," replied Yūichi. After wiping his hands briefly, he started across the pier towards Mr. Caan's home.

In the middle of the pier he stopped, without reason, and turned back toward Mr. Caan.

Mr. Caan was staring at the sea, absent-mindedly smoking a cigarette. He was wearing a tired face: unusual for him. His skin sagged, there were circles under his eyes—it was, to be blunt, an old face.

Yūichi, feeling he had seen something bad, glanced away automatically. *Why is Mr. Caan that tired? It's so unlike him*, he wondered.

▲

Yūichi didn't dislike driving an EV manually, either.

True, when he was driving with the car on manual, all the people quietly zipping along the Electronic Control Highway looked like fools. They looked like a herd of sheep. For excitement, anyway, the EV was a far call from a rocket propulsion submersible. It wasn't a question of speed: the EV was much faster.... It was a question of how you felt about it.

And so, when he set the car on the Electronic Control Highway, and pushed the dashboard buttons to select the destination, he felt relieved.

After that, the automatic system would take over driving, delivering him to his destination by the least-crowded route. The driver could sleep, or read a book, or do whatever he liked.

Today, especially, Yūichi didn't feel like driving.

He was carrying an important cargo. If by some chance there were an accident, an apology just wouldn't do.

Mr. Caan's wife.

Mrs. Caan was a small, red-haired woman. She was over twenty years younger than he, beautiful, and had something ultra-special about her. Which is not to say that she was snobbish.

At parties, she always played the sparkling hostess. Her laughing voice was bright and clear—she was a good match for Mr. Caan.

She was a genuine lady.

Most ladies weren't given to vast self-expression, and she made little effort to express her own emotions, perhaps because it seemed unproductive. Mrs. Caan always held her head up straight, a little proudly even, with a subtle smile. She never, never revealed an angry or excited face to the world.

2018 :: Age 18

Still, Mrs. Caan had few words today, and somehow seemed drained. She faced absolutely forward, and her lips held their same delicate smile; but it seemed a little forced, a little unnatural.

For Mr. and Mrs. Caan both to show such tired faces, so unusual for them, naturally worried Yūichi, but as a mere boat boy, he could hardly ask what was wrong.

If he asked they would probably tell him, but he figured it would be better not to ask at all.

Eighteen years old was hardly the age of a simple child.

The gentle, faintly sweet smell of oleander was drifting through the car.

Yūichi couldn't judge if it was real oleander, or the perfume Mrs. Caan was wearing.

While he was wondering about it, he silently looked at the map displayed on the car's display screen.

A bright point of light on the screen showed that the EV would arrive at the airport in less than ten minutes.

"A toy, . . ." she said to herself, quietly.

"Huh?"

"This road is a toy," she said, as if speaking to herself. Then she asked Yūichi "Don't you agree?"

"Mm . . . I don't know. . . ."

"Do you like it?"

"I love it."

"You love it like your very own toy, right?"

"That's right, Ma'am." Yūichi laughed briefly. "But I've never thought of it that way before. Why do you say it like that?"

"When I see the Electronic Control Highway, I laugh." With a slightly absent-minded gesture, she patted her hair. Her hair, brushed but unstyled, had become a little disorderly in the breeze.

"This road is what I was told all roads of the future would look like...."

"But aren't all roads like this now?"

"Was Tokyo the same?"

"Tokyo's roads are... bad. They can't be compared."

"There aren't any electronic highways in Tokyo, are there?"

"No, that's right. There are air-cushion vehicles."

"Air-cushion vehicles..."

As if confirming something to herself, she said "These days they're all the same. Air cushion vehicles. Air-cushion vehicles are economical and absolutely safe...."

"But..." Yūichi interrupted her, hesitated, then spoke out. "I like electric cars so much more than air-cushion cars. You can see outside, and you can tell you're moving."

After a pause, she said quietly, "My husband said the same thing."

"And don't you think the same way?"

"I don't know."

"Mm..."

"But when you say this road is your toy, though, I feel I understand."

"Because men and women are different."

"True." Her voice was flat, but a strange undertone of coldness was in it. "Men and women are different."

With that, she fell silent. She took dark sunglasses from her bag, and put them on. Her ever-present smile began to dance... suddenly she was an unknown, approachable woman.

2018 :: Age 18

Yūichi was troubled. He felt he had said something unneeded, or not said enough, and was uncomfortable, but he had no choice but to fall silent as well.

The EV slid into the airport terminal, and came silently to a stop.

"Thank you," she said to Yūichi, who was unloading her luggage from the car. "I can get a robo-porter from here, so it's all right. . . ."

"When will you be returning, Ma'am?" he asked, without thinking.

"Mm . . ." She looked straight at him. With the dark sunglasses and smile, he couldn't see her expression. It was as if she were wearing a mask.

"My husband knows," she said, before long. "Ask him." Turning her back to Yūichi, she walked off toward the glidewalk. It was exactly as if the world opened a path for her as she left.

Afterwards, only the indistinct smell of oleander remained.

"So it was her perfume, after all, . . ." realized Yūichi, slowly. He felt a premonition that something like this would happen to him again, someday.

He couldn't understand why he felt that way.

3

YŪICHI DIRECTED THE EV to Herself sector.

He inserted his all-credit card into its dashboard slot, and attached the bill to Mr. Caan's account. Then, after pushing the "park" button, he got out.

The car, like a clever horse, ran off in search of its next customer. Yūichi watched it go for a while, and then slowly lifted his eyes. Here, the nerve center of Aphrodite spread out around him—not only the Control and Information Towers, but different types of marine research installations, museums and public buildings, high-class hotels for tourists, and the largest shopping center in the city.

Yūichi felt overpowered by it all every time he set foot in Herself.

To Yūichi, who had grown up in Tokyo, big cities weren't that scary. Simply in terms of size, Herself couldn't hold a candle to Tokyo. From the money angle, too, Tokyo had many more expensive buildings. It was foolish to even try to compare them.

Still, he was overpowered by Herself; he felt his breath taken away, because it offered a geometrical beauty not imaginable in Tokyo: functional beauty taken to the pinnacle.

Perhaps it was the ideal of beauty as the product of human hands. That metallic beauty couldn't be seen elsewhere. Though it was made of ultra-alloys and plastics—no, probably exactly *because* it was made that way—Herself sector made you feel, more than anywhere else, warm.

Like all the other sectors of Aphrodite, Herself was nothing more than special frames wrapped around floating module core-towers, complicated high-rise modules, and plazas. Still, when the vertical shafts, platforms, structural and equipment floors, observation decks, and various types of towers were all gathered close, and bound together organically with a monorail, the entire thing became, suddenly, sheer beauty. Such was Herself sector.

When it was under sunlight, glittering Herself flashed like a mirage of reflected light. At night, with the lamps of the VTOL buses and the lights of the roads strung together like beads, the area was transformed, bejeweled.

In fact, Herself was where the ultra-modern metropolis and—although the phrase was trite— the "Paradise of the South Seas" met: here was the place that held all the charm of Aphrodite, and the strangeness.

Of course Yūichi loved to visit Herself. It was, for him, an experience more exciting than any other.

Even so, he didn't want to live there. He would hate it. It was far better to live in Herleg, or if not there, then in Herhip, he thought. He felt that you couldn't get friendly with Herself, couldn't touch it.

He didn't really understand why, and he hadn't really thought about it. He imagined vaguely that it was the same reason that Mr. Caan didn't choose to live in Herself.

YŪICHI GOT ON A high-speed elevator, and shot up to the observation deck.

2018 :: Age 18

He didn't have any particular business in Herself. He just came to enjoy himself, making the best of an unexpected break. Herself lacked nothing in the way of fun.

The observation deck was crowded: everyone was lost in the blue of the ocean that stretched out beyond the glass panels, mouthing expressions of astonishment, like children. Most of them were tourists, and two Japanese couples were mixed in with the rest.

Yūichi felt no desire to watch the sea beyond the glass panels. As he began to retrace his steps, thinking maybe he would go see a 3D movie, he was stopped by a voice from behind.

"Hey, it's Yūichi!" It was a low, throbbing voice, baritone, and a voice he remembered. Before he turned, he knew whose voice it was.

"Hi!" Yūichi turned, smiling.

Voight was standing there, a young man with black hair and a thin face that made you think "Asian." He was always quiet, never tried raising his voice. He could be trusted.

Voight was the only son of the publisher of a progressive newspaper called the *Aphrodite Facsimile*. He also wanted to be a journalist, and he was majoring in Media Communications at the University. They said he was a genius at it.

Voight's father also had a rocket-propelled submersible, and that was how they met and became friends.

"No work today?" Voight asked.

"Nope." Yūichi shook his head, asking in return, "No school for you?"

"No, I've got school. . . . But a girl relative of mine came to have fun, so I'm showing her the sights of

Aphrodite for the day. I'll introduce you.... Hey, over here!"

His last words were not directed at Yūichi, but at someone mixed in with the tourists.

A single girl split off from the tourist group, and came walking over to them. The instant he saw her, a charge strong enough to light a hundred-watt bulb surged through his body. In his head, the jackpot bell of a slot machine was ringing.

He felt as if a blinding radiance had appeared in front of his eyes. His heart pounded.... Loose blonde hair, hazel eyes, plump lips ... To Yūichi, she was perfection incarnate.

She was just on the verge of womanhood, full of vitality and life. Like a young puppy that can't stand still for even a minute, she couldn't hold back the sheer happiness at being alive, bubbling up from deep inside her.

It was only his first impression, and you had to be careful with first impressions, but he had fallen in love with her at first sight... and he had to say she certainly was a stunning beauty.

Love at first sight? Yes, even in this day and age, the phenomenon of love at first sight still survived, somehow. Medicine had finally advanced to controlling cancer, but it hadn't been able to make a drug against this malady.

Voight, without seeming to notice Yūichi's agitation, brought them together and introduced them.

Her name was Anita. A name with a good ring to it.

"I've already guided her through most of Herself, and I was thinking of going to Herhip next," said Voight. "Why don't you come along?"

"Let me see...." Yūichi pretended to think, and then nodded. "OK. Be happy to!"

2018 :: Age 18

"Oh, good!" Anita laughed innocently. "This is my first trip to Aphrodite. I always love making new friends!"

Really, those words are bad for my heart, he thought.

▲

APHRODITE HAD THE SHAPE of a spiral seashell, flaring outward.

Seen from above, Herhead was a small swelling, and Aphrodite became roughly horseshoe-shaped. Herself was in the center, to the east was Herleg sector, and Herhip sector was to the west.

The Electronic Control Highway ran through and networked the three sectors; you could also use the regular hydrofoil service to cross the central bay. Both were very fast.

Still, if you didn't have any especially urgent business, absolutely the first thing to do was to walk along the Ocean Promenade. This was a plastic tube suspended about ten meters below the surface of the ocean, running in an almost straight line across the bay—out of the way of the ship traffic, of course.

When Aphrodite moved, the Ocean Promenade was quickly withdrawn by marine robots. No problem.

To human eyes, the ocean at ten meters down was superbly beautiful. It was full of the sun's radiance.

Silver bubbles formed chains, rising to burst on the ocean's surface, flashing just above your head. Every kind of fish swam past the sides of the Promenade: slowly, elegantly. Beautiful but nameless jellyfish, anemones, and unknown spiky things crawled slowly along the rock surface. The vivid colors of the coral reef were like something out of a dream. Occasionally, a shape flashed past overhead, casting a dark shadow: a dolphin, no doubt.

People who walked the Ocean Promenade were always surprised to discover that the sea was full of sound.

The smashing waves, the long wavelengths of the crying ocean, could be heard from somewhere; the sound of darting shrimp, the speech of dolphins, and even the words of the sharks were all picked up by underwater microphones, and transmitted to the listening ear—a symphony.

Of course there was a glide-walk running through the Ocean Promenade, and people arrived at their destinations while chasing the fish with their eyes and listening to the symphony. It was very comfortable.

Some people preferred to walk through the Ocean Promenade on their own feet. Sidewalks had been constructed on both sides of the glide-walk, and the three young friends strolled slowly along. Nobody was in a particular hurry.

Every time a fish came close, Anita screamed, laughed. Her cheeks were flushed with excitement.

Now, finding something ahead, Anita ran forward thirty meters, and pressed her forehead against the plastic wall. Voight and Yūichi looked at each other, and shared faint smiles.

"She's just a kid," said Voight, as if apologizing. "She's still just a kid."

"Uh-huh." Yūichi nodded, and chuckled.

Like a little child, Anita came running back. As if making a proclamation, she announced: "I'll never forget today! I mean . . . Wow! This is so great!"

Yūichi thought, deep in his heart, that he would

2018 :: Age 18

never forget the beauty of her eyes, flashing brightly with excitement.

HERHIP SECTOR HAD A completely different flavor from Herleg or Herself.

It was all a jumble. Narrow. Noisy. A little smelly—the smell of oil, the smell of anti-perspirant, the smells of cooking meat and fish: all mixed up together, brewing a special odor all of its own. Roads came together, ended abruptly, and stone steps were thrown in for good measure, and somehow it all seemed like a maze. Nobody paid any attention to "city planning." People had built the roads in whatever manner pleased them, and as a result it was an amoeba-like, shapeless, unorganized place.

People said it resembled the Arab quarter of Paris, but of course it was home to more than Arabs.

Herhip was Mr. Caan's immigrant quarter, in the real sense of the word. The phrase "Crucible of Humanity" just wasn't strong enough to encompass it: if you put all the people of the world in a pot, and boiled them, and stirred them with your hand, and made them into a dumpling—that would be Herhip.

It was all true. In this area, if your next-door neighbor was a Yeti nobody would be at all surprised. It was doubtful anyone would be surprised to bump into an alien monster.

Some people on the island demanded that Herhip sector be dismantled. Herhip was home to pickpockets and petty thieves, and knife-fights were not unusual. There was prostitution of all sorts, male and female. Morphine and heroin weren't that common, but hallucinogens were sold publicly. It wasn't nice, and so it should be removed at once.

There was another point, though, that the "dismantle Herhip" advocates had against them in convincing people; and although they were always steering around the issue, it was public knowledge: the people living in Herhip weren't there because they were poor.

In Aphrodite, with its highly-advanced welfare system, it was possible to rent even an elegant house in Herleg for almost nothing. In fact, there were many vacant houses there. The people living in Herhip could move at any time, but they stayed because they liked it. It appealed to them.

Why?

There was more to Herhip sector than shoplifters and fights and prostitution. It offered the true meaning of the words "energy" and "life." There was the smell of humanity laughing, crying, living—things that you couldn't hope to find in Herself, of course, but neither could you find them in Herleg.

Even Yūichi, who loathed disorderly Tokyo, and should have loved Herleg sector, thought it would be OK to live in Herhip.

No, while both Herhip and Tokyo were disorderly and seemed to resemble each other superficially, he thought they were absolute opposites at heart.

Herhip was like a very hot spice. It stung the tongue, and was hot enough to make your eyes water, but you couldn't stop yourself from licking it to get a taste. In comparison, Tokyo was artificial, chemical flavoring—neither was very good for your health, but an ordinary person would, no mistake, choose the spice.

The stone walkways of Herhip and the sidewalks of Tokyo both seemed to be eternally dirty, but Her-

2018 :: Age 18

hip's stones were dirty with fish oil, while Tokyo's sidewalks were dirtied with plastic litter. That was how Yūichi felt. It was a pleasure just to walk to the harbor in Herhip.

There, especially there, all kinds of ships were moored, from engined ships to junks. Nobody in Aphrodite would starve if the fish catch failed, but for the people here, it seemed to be a sin not to catch fish from the sea in front of them. You could say they chose to live in Herhip just because they were that type of person.

When you saw the prows of the ships lined up at their moorings, ships that might have come from a museum, the illusion carried you back, somehow, centuries into the past. Walking on the wet paving stones, listening to the bickering banter between the sailors and the bargirls, you felt a chest-tightening nostalgia.

Lifting your eyes from the port and looking across to the opposite side, you could see the jumbled line of houses—churches built next to mosques, and so on. No, while it certainly was jumbled, even that disorder seemed to possess a strange kind of harmony.

Vulgar, wanton, and—above all—authentic: that was Herhip.

The three of them walked along the harbor, stuffing their mouths with food from a street café.

Fish cooked in some way—boiled, baked, fried: who knew?—wrapped in a chapati, drenched in grease, and too hot to hold. If you closed your eyes a little to the mess, they were incredibly delicious, and incredibly cheap—for the three of them, it was lunch.

At first, Anita was a little hesitant about the atmosphere of Herhip, but at last came to like it.

As they finished eating their chapatis, she darted her eyes here and there in the town, and started to run again.

Impulsively, she bought three ice creams from a street vendor and brought them back looking ecstatic.

Anita was enjoying Herhip from the bottom of her heart.

"You eat like that and your stomach doesn't hurt?" teased Voight.

"Me, I can eat eight pieces of toast," said Anita seriously. "When I feel really good, even ten is a breeze."

They walked as far as the edge of the harbor, and climbed up a narrow, winding street. At the top of the street was a small restaurant bar: the Laugh Cat, where Yūichi and his friends always hung out.

THE LAUGH CAT'S MANAGER was named Tarloff.

He had a receding hairline, and the top of his head was smooth as an egg. His long sideburns connected up with his beard, making it look like his face was sewed on. Every time he laughed in his deep voice his protruding belly shook like jelly, and he looked old—he had only just turned forty, though.

"What? You ruffians? And in the daytime?" When he saw Yūichi and Voight enter the Laugh Cat, Tarloff burst forth with that huge voice, but when Anita followed them in his eyes bulged in surprise. "Ah! A rare sight! A beautiful woman for a guest!" For this middle-aged valiant, these should have been words of the highest praise, but he brayed them out loud to the point of rudeness.

Anita tightened her cheeks, and looked primly to

2018 :: Age 18

one side. Still, she wasn't really mad: her eyes were laughing.

Tarloff set bottles of beer in front of Yūichi and Voight, and, looking at Anita, stood thinking with his lips protruding a little. Finally, he brought out another bottle of beer. Then he turned to the kitchen, and called out in a loud voice; "Three tuna steaks!"

From the kitchen, a woman's face glanced out. It was his daughter: seventeen-year-old Sue. Tarloff called her his niece, but everyone knew that she was really his daughter by a Chinese woman he had fallen in love with when he was younger. Her eyes were provocatively large and black, with high cheekbones and slightly dark skin. She was a stunning beauty, but for some reason she didn't try to mix with the customers—she wasn't drawn to it, perhaps, or maybe it was just a pain. She made no effort to leave the kitchen except when she was serving.

"Three orders of tuna steak," said Tarloff, as if to remind her, and Sue's face withdrew back into the kitchen.

Yūichi drew from the bottle in gulps, and wiped the foam off his lips with the back of his hand. Then he stole a glance at Anita, seated to the side. Anita was timidly sipping a glass of beer. It looked like this was her first time to drink beer, too.

Yūichi tried out various sentences in his head. All no good. He wanted to strike up a conversation, but everything he thought of sounded so contrived. Not polished enough . . . He looked over to Voight for help.

Voight was gazing into the distance, relaxed, sipping his beer. *That bastard has no sense of friendship. Even silence has its limits. . . . .*

Yūichi, feeling cornered, suddenly stood and

walked over to the old jukebox standing in a corner of the room. He dropped in a coin, and chose a tune.

For an instant there was silence, then the sounds of a record being set—a needle scratching across an old disk, sighing for a few seconds—then the wild chords of a guitar echoed through the Laugh Cat.

> *Believe me, baby*
> *Me, well, me*
> *I'm like I am now*
> *I ain't gonna be no GI*
> *I ain't gonna be no white-collar*
> *I ain't gonna be no egghead*
> *I ain't gonna be no salesman*
> *Me, I'm gonna be me*
> *So, you see*
> *Me, I'm gonna be me*
> *I'm just like I am now*
> *I'm gonna love you forever*
> *So come on, baby*
> *Let's love*
> *Take off that little triangle of cloth*

It was the voice of the Aphrodite Kid. The Kid was a unique singer, somehow managing to become a star without anyone ever seeing his face, without ever giving a stage or 3D show.

His songs, his words, and music, too, were rough and unfinished, but they always made his listeners happy, grabbing your heartstrings.

The street-talk said the Kid was from Aphrodite—which is precisely why his songs were received so fanatically by the youth of Aphrodite—but his recordings were sold worldwide, and always took the top spots on the charts.

2018 :: Age 18

The Kid was a hero to Aphrodite's youth, the symbol of their adolescence.

Yūichi, swinging his hips just a little, returned to his seat, and asked, in as relaxed a voice as he could manage, "Dance?"

Anita looked a bit surprised, and flashed a quick look at Voight, but when she saw him nod, she stood up enthusiastically. Her cheeks were flushed and her eyes flashed, sparkled.

Beautiful . . . How many times have I said that today? Yūichi thought as he looked at Anita.

The two of them, still facing each other, moved out to the center of the dance floor. There, they stopped quietly and caught each other's eyes—as Tarloff's loud laugh came across to them.

Yūichi stuck his chest forward, Anita swayed her shoulders and twisted her hips, riding the music.

Three steps forward, two to the side. Step, step, clap.

> *Believe me, baby*
> *I ain't goin' nowhere*
> *I wanna stay here*

Anita shifted her hips, and faced Yūichi with her arms spread, as if she would come attacking. Her blond hair was shining, and her skirt flared. Her long, slender legs tapped on the floor, and her dry fingers echoed like castanets.

Turn, then step, step.

> *New York, it's a trashcan*
> *Paris, an old folks home*
> *London's a museum*
> *Tokyo's a loonie bin*

Their movements accelerated. Like the shadow cast by a spinning mirror, Anita's figure shattered into fragments and vanished from Yūichi's sight. He leaned back slightly and continued to step in time.

Front, front, side, side . . . and, in time with the recording, he too burst into song.

> *This is the tops*
> *That's right*
> *This is the very tops*
> *I wanna stay here*
> *I'm gonna love you forever*

Suddenly Yūichi felt his collar grabbed from behind. Yanked away, he almost lost his balance, barely managing to right himself. By the time he did, someone had already cut in, and was partnering Anita.

Anita had been taken from him silently, masterfully. "I'm Gil. I'm one of their friends." She heard the newcomer's introduction, and, relieved, began to dance again.

Gil winked at Yūichi, as if to say "Forgive me!" Then, with a sly smile, began to dance.

> *So come on, baby*
> *Let's love*
> *Down that beer, all you want*

Yūichi, stunned, just kept standing there. It took him a minute to figure out what had happened.

True, Gil was one of their friends. He also worked as a boat boy, for a French technician. A tall, clumsy-looking guy with a long face, he looked like a laughing horse when he showed his white teeth.

2018 :: Age 18

Even though he had those comical features, he had a sharp tongue; sometimes his calmly spoken words cut to the heart. But people didn't hate him much, because he was, strangely enough, an affectionate, good-tempered person.

Yūichi, too, liked Gil. He felt more relaxed mixing with Gil than he did with the slightly more mature Voight. Still . . .

Still, . . . thought Yūichi, as he felt his anger come bubbling up, *there were limits. Even to being a smart-ass. Goddamn son of a bitch. . . .*

4

A MILD BREEZE WAS blowing.

In the pitch-black depths of the sea, it flickered: a silver streak, rising. The silver streak rose gradually, finally morphing into triangular waves, and they came tumbling down.

The sound of rolling, crashing surf . . . a booming breaker, the rustle of withdrawing foam . . .

A full moon hung in the sky, and the horizon was painted in radiance, glittering like the back of a fish.

Yūichi sat on the end of the pier, and lazily watched the sea.

The breeze blowing from the sea had a faintly sweet smell. He had smelled it somewhere before, but he couldn't recall what it was.

The murmur of laughing voices came from some party at a house. Yūichi felt gloomy somehow. When the close of the day grew near, his mood always darkened. It was like sad remembrances of his youth, watching the sandcastles he built by the sea gradually slipping into the waves.

Sitting alone like this, Yūichi thought of what the future might bring, vaguely, with a mixture of hope and unease, and he felt a kind of foreboding. In five years, in ten years, where would he be, and what would he be doing? Who would he meet . . . he couldn't help questioning himself.

He shrugged, and shifted his eyes to the view of Herleg behind him.

The lights of the houses twinkled like a constellation in the lavender dimness. Those lights were something very precious to him, and he couldn't stop himself from gazing for long minutes at Herleg.

Behind him, the sounds of the crashing sea suddenly echoed loudly. Yūichi turned, and felt his melancholy vanish from his heart in the next instant, as if a switch had turned off. The vital happiness he had felt during the day was suddenly reborn.... Yūichi was, by nature, not much of an introvert.

A rocket-propelled submersible floated in the sea twenty meters from the pier. The pilot was almost certainly Gil.

Of course, it went without saying that he had borrowed the submersible without the permission of his French employer.

Yūichi lightly jumped up, and sprang to the deck of the *Rosebud*. Opening the hatch, he lithely twisted his body and slid into the seat. As he grasped the controls, he felt power come bubbling up inside him.

He felt a little bad about borrowing the *Rosebud* without asking Mr. Caan, but he was only going to borrow it this once, tonight. Maybe if he told himself it was just a replacement for running tests, he wouldn't feel like such a criminal.

With practised hands, Yūichi finished checking the main ballast tanks, trim tanks, propulsion system, and the rest. Lastly, he switched on the television camera, and angled the variable thruster to different vectors—everything was *Go!*

He put on the earphones and fine-tuned the radio.

"Finished your checks?" Before Yūichi could

2018 :: Age 18

speak, Gil's high-pitched voice echoed in his earphones.

"Yeah," Yūichi said, nodding. "I'm *go* anytime."

Yūichi's voice was totally serious. He was serious, and in a corner of his heart he felt a tiny bit of brightness, and lightness.

Yūichi and Gil, just the two of them, had decided to settle the matter of a first date with Anita by a submersible race.

The rules were very simple—they would start their submersibles at the same time, and the first to pass under Aphrodite and surface on the far side would win the honor of the first date with Anita.

Of course, it was just fun. Still, you couldn't say it was *only* fun. To the eighteen-year-old Yūichi and Gil, everything was fun—and was worth pursuing seriously, as an all-out effort.

Yūichi started up *Rosebud's* surface propulsion, and moved up roughly even with the craft that Gil was piloting.

He could see a small school of flurried fish through the tiny peep window at his feet, lit up by the lights.

"When I count to three, start." Gil's voice echoed through the earphones a second time. "One... Two..."

By the time he heard three, Yūichi had already submerged the *Rosebud*.

In an instant, the bubbly surface crossed the television screen, and the *Rosebud* slipped into the sea on a slight forward plane. As it passed fifty meters in depth, the control thrusters kicked in, protecting the balance of the weight and buoyancy.

When Gil's submersible vanished from the television screen, Yūichi was a little bit confused. He felt a doubt... Was Gil's craft so advanced that the *Rosebud* just couldn't match it?

He was instantly relieved when he saw that Gil had simply taken a shallower course, but at the same time his determination flared anew.

Gil might have been playing a little dirty, but he was playing to win. For Gil, it marked an extraordinary tenacity regarding Anita.

Well, Yūichi felt the same when it came to wanting to win this race more than anything.

One second, two seconds... Almost grinding his teeth, Yūichi waited for the rocket engine power to build up. He could almost hear the fuel being pumped from the tank to the bypass.

He slammed the main engine lever forward with all his strength.

It was a violent start. No mistake, anyone who started a submersible like that during a licensing test would be failed right there—no avoiding it. Somehow, the water in front of Yūichi had been cut open by Gil's wake.

The submersible, like a stone hurled from a catapult, sprang through the water.

Yūichi thought that he definitely heard the *Rosebud's* body creaking. For an instant he lost it, and thought he heard water leaking in from somewhere, but of course no submersible would be damaged by this kind of treatment.

The television camera finally caught Gil's submersible.

Gil's craft was quite far ahead, but not so far he couldn't overtake him. The giant free-floating foundations supporting the ballast tank and engine room of Aphrodite, the level water that doubled as sea lanes were intricate, like the frame of a building.

2018 :: Age 18

It was an obstacle race. With skill you could win back any distance.

The free-floating bases came rushing towards him on the television screen. He felt as if a small mountain was falling towards him. At this speed, if he didn't pay attention to what he was doing, he would end up running smack into a foundation. As that occurred to him he took the long way around, opening up even more distance, and so fell even further behind Gil.

Yūichi circled well around, avoiding the free-floating foundation. The supporting columns cut triangular shadows on his television screen: a complex weave, like a cat's cradle.

Yūichi continued to play the control thrusters. The *Rosebud* twisted like a dolphin, and threaded between the support pillars. *Superb technique!* Yūichi gave a short laugh when he saw that the distance to Gil's submersible had shortened visibly. In avoiding the columns, Gil seemed to have lost a little headway.

Of course, he shouldn't get too excited about leaping merely the first hurdle.

The number of free-floating foundations, stretches of level water, and pillars needed to support Aphrodite, which itself supported a population of two hundred thousand, was beyond imagination. There were countless hurdles left to jump.

Yūichi felt cold sweat on his hands, grasping the control stick. Moving under Aphrodite at any speed, let alone racing at top speed ... Well, it was pretty crazy. Yūichi finally noticed he was risking his life. But, strangely, he felt no desire to stop the race now.

Naturally, it was nothing more than a joking contest to see who would date Anita first. Still, even in spite of that—no, maybe especially because of that—he didn't feel like stopping the race in the middle.

The next free-floating foundation was approaching. *God Damn, it was big....* He unconsciously wanted to open up the space between him and it as much as possible. The cowardly child in Yūichi was screaming, crying, but he left only the bare minimum of space as he cut around the foundation and threaded through the triangular shapes of the support columns.

In this type of situation, you had to force your reflexes to learn new tricks. If you hesitated like an amateur, it would only be more dangerous.

This time, Yūichi didn't laugh.

The distance between his craft and Gil's hadn't shortened at all. No mistake, Gil had mastered the right timing, too.

The next foundation, and then the one after that... The *Rosebud*, somehow, continued to leap her hurdles.

It was the kind of race that wore on the nerves—incredibly so. Yūichi's face was white, but at the same time he was savoring his success because he had never before piloted a submersible so freely.

It felt so *different* to race through the ocean. The speed wasn't much different from that of a sub, but his craft was small, and that made the sensation of speed a new dimension entirely. It made driving an EV on land seem like child's play.

Yūichi felt himself relax a little, although only a little bit. He was in tune, now. All he had to do now was draw on his technique, and concentrate on shaving off the centimeters between his submersible and Gil's.

2018 :: Age 18

It would be cruel to say that this relaxation in Yūichi's thinking was an invitation to disaster. There was an accident was waiting to happen, and happen it did.

Yūichi again felt himself losing the ability to control the *Rosebud*. The control thrusters stopped having any effect.

He didn't know why.

How to say it . . . It felt like a giant, unseen hand had grabbed the *Rosebud*, and was trying to pull her down to the sea bottom.

It happened in a flash.

There was no time even to be afraid.

When he noticed it, Yūichi stared fixedly, unblinking, at the support pillar that came rushing directly at him in the television screen.

In the next instant, a shock threw him free of the pilot's seat.

Of course, this was also Yūichi's first experience of losing consciousness.

WHEN MR. CAAN STEPPED into the hospital room, both Yūichi and Gil were sitting on the edge of their beds, blankly wasting time.

After such intense effort, that seething sense of exultation, despondency always comes—that, and the fact that they still couldn't tell if they were being kept in the hospital as patients or as criminals. . . .

Yūichi didn't even know what had happened to the two of them. When he had come to, he was already in the hospital, getting an EEG. He was vastly relieved when he was told that it was only a slight concussion, but the doctor made no effort to answer any questions beyond that. He wasn't just pretending ignorance: he really didn't know.

After the doctors left, Gil and Yūichi exchanged information in a frenzy, but in the end they only found out that both of their submersibles had met with some kind of accident.

Yūichi and Gil, crestfallen, sat with drooping shoulders, staring blankly at the floor. Just two kids who had done something bad and were being made to stay after school.

And that was when Mr. Caan came into the hospital room.

He didn't look particularly mad: merely a little—well—interested.

"Is the *Rosebud* all right?" questioned Yūichi, as soon as he saw Mr. Caan's figure. It seemed that was bothering him the most.

"There's just a little damage to the hull," nodded Mr. Caan, and added, without special emphasis, "You would be . . . Gil? . . . I just met your boss. He says you're fired."

Gil, looking like a horse with its feed bag taken away, turned expressionless.

"I wonder about me. . . ."

To Yūichi's question, Mr. Caan slowly turned to face him, and counter-questioned, "Do you want to be fired?"

"Of course not!" Yūichi laughed loudly.

"In that case, it's all right for you to keep working for me, just like before. . . ."

". . . ."

Yūichi felt relief spreading throughout his body. If he had been forbidden to ride a submersible any more, what would he do to live tomorrow? He hadn't found an answer—his relief was too strong, and he lost any room in his heart for empathy with his friend, who had just become jobless.

2018 :: Age 18

"Why?" asked Yūichi, finally. "I used the *Rosebud* without permission. You're not going to get angry?"

"If only my boss understood us like Mr. Caan does, . . ." whispered Gil, close to complaining.

"Understand you kids?" Mr. Caan's voice held a laugh. "That's a joke! What are you saying? If I weren't the mayor of Aphrodite, I'd be firing Yūichi right now. Naturally! Never forget, you two, children and adults are two different species. It's the normal state of things for us to be snarling at each other."

"Then why?" Yūichi asked the same question, this time nervously.

"Because to preserve the energy of Aphrodite as our home, she needs people like you, too," answered Mr. Caan.

"Not to mention impulsive teenagers," he went on. "Why do think I allowed manual driving in Herhip sector? Because I don't want to make Aphrodite into a *finished* place. People can't live in totally finished worlds. It is a city, and yet it isn't. It's something else again. . . . People aren't such high-class animals. They can't live in a true utopia. An incomplete utopia—that's the best environment of all. Not to mention, the city only functions this well exactly *because* it has such atypical elements. You kids are sort of a stimulant, energizing Aphrodite. . . ."

". . . ."

Suddenly, Yūichi had nothing to say. He thought that maybe Mr. Caan didn't love anyone: it was clear that what he loved was Aphrodite.

"Hmm . . . Speaking of incomplete elements, the whirlpool that caught you two—we call it the giant whirlpool—that's another one."

Mr. Caan spoke as if recalling something. "Maybe

it's because of Aphrodite's heat output, or maybe because of some tidal current, but that whirlpool keeps appearing. And every time, its energy grows greater. I only hope it doesn't finally destroy Aphrodite. That, especially that, is an incomplete element we could do without. . . ." Mr. Caan waved his hand slightly, a motion to indicate the end of his talk. Then he turned his heel and started to leave the room.

"Uh . . . When should I go to the airport to pick up your wife, sir?" Yūichi himself had no idea why he chose to ask such a question then. Almost automatically, he opened his mouth and the words came out.

Mr. Caan turned, slowly. He was in the shadow of the light, and Yūichi couldn't see his expression.

"She won't be coming back." Then, in a strangely level voice, he added "According to her, my wife is Aphrodite. I don't need two wives, she said. So, she left."

After Mr. Caan left the room, Yūichi and Gil looked at each other. At the same instant, they both released their held breath.

After Yūichi returned to his own room and was taking a shower, he got a videophone call.

"What in the hell happened?" asked Voight. "I heard you and Gil got hurt. Scared the hell out of me!"

"Nothing much. . . . Just a bump."

"Well, that's OK then. . . . Anyway, today's a special day for me. Two of my best friends getting banged up spoils it a bit, though. . . ."

"Special day?"

"Mm . . . Anita and I, we got engaged."

2018 :: Age 18

"..."

"Hello? Hello?"

"... I hear you. But aren't you and Anita related?"

"Only very distant relatives. Genetically, there's no problem at all."

"Ah. I see."

"Hey, it's the truth!"

"Congrats," said Yūichi.

After he hung up, Yūichi rolled into bed, still wet from the shower. He lay looking up at the ceiling, and finally he began to chuckle.

What a day! What an incredible day....

As he was laughing, he felt signs of sleepiness: guess I am worn out, after all, he thought.

Yūichi shut his eyes, and slept.... A slight smile hovering on his sleeping face.

2023 :: Age 23

▲▲▲▲   1

YŪICHI OPENED HIS EYES.

He stared steadily at the dark ceiling. He didn't know why he had woken up.

There was only the vague remnant of a bittersweet memory lingering in his mind.

For a while, he gave himself over to trying to recall that memory.

The room wasn't pitch-black. Faint moonlight was seeping in through the blinds. It was slightly bluish, and had the transparency of fine crystal.

As if suddenly remembering something, Yūichi twisted his neck and checked the clock at the side of his pillow.

3:00 A.M. . .

Of course, it wasn't time to get up, and as Yūichi was a sound sleeper, it was unlikely he would wake up in the middle of the night without a reason.

From the bed he listened carefully, trying to determine what had awakened him.

It was quiet.

Except for the sound of the waves, he could hear nothing.

After a while, a yawn leaked out, he rolled over, and tried to reenter the land of dreams.

That was when he heard the shouting.

It sounded like a continuous, distant roar, and it

wasn't just one or two people. There were dozens of people shouting, screaming, occasionally punctuated by a loud, dry sound. The sound of riot guns.

This time, for sure, Yūichi was wide awake. He sprang up, leaping out of bed. The night air felt tingling cool on his naked torso, but now wasn't the time to worry about something like that.

Suddenly, a brilliant light came blazing through the window, into Yūichi's eyes. The room was painted with the pattern of the horizontal blinds.

Yūichi blinked his eyes, and put his hand on the windowsill through a crack in the blinds, and opened the window with one push. Then he shut it, fast. He had smelled the sweet, slightly minty scent of tranquilizer gas. When your nerves were suppressed by that gas, you drooled, grinned idiotically, and felt deliriously happy: it lasted for twenty-four hours. You lost all your will power.

No mistake, the police and the demonstrators were colliding here, now, right in Herleg.

Angry shouts and screams could be heard in succession. It might have been his imagination, but he thought he also heard the dull echoes of blows on flesh. For the time being, Yūichi entered the bathroom, wet a towel with water, and pressed it to his nose.

As long as you didn't get a healthy whiff, there was no worry of being tranquilized.

He sat on the edge of the bed, downcast, and decided to wait for the disturbance to fade away.

Demonstrations were common here in Aphrodite, or rather in Herleg. Their ringleaders were mostly teenagers, loudly and unreservedly demanding the retirement of the Mayor, Mr. Caan. According to them, he was a coward eating up all the finances of

2023 :: Age 23

Aphrodite, a schemer in the shadows, and, above all, selfishly devoted to his own gratification.

Naturally, Yūichi couldn't agree with their opinions. As he didn't agree, he thought it wasn't a serious complaint, and he despised them.

Part of that was natural because Yūichi was employed by Mr. Caan, and revered him, but that wasn't all—he didn't notice it himself, but Yūichi was no longer young.

At twenty-three, Yūichi wasn't young?

Better to say that Yūichi was no longer young enough.

The future had limitless possibilities, and to the teenagers for whom it shone and sparkled, it was the so very near future. Twenty . . . twenty-one . . . twenty-two . . . as you grew older, your life grew less colorful, and the solidity of reality came to nest. When that reality came pressing, and forced Yūichi to make a decision, Yūichi's life came to have that much more pressure: it became stifling.

Yūichi had, it's true, succeeded in getting his license for rocket-propelled submersibles. But even as he was ecstatic about finally getting it, he had to face the merciless reality that you couldn't eat a submersible license—and here on Aphrodite, less than a hundred people actually had rocket submersibles. He might have the license, but it wasn't going to do him much good. . . .

Yūichi could hardly stay on as Mr. Caan's boat boy forever. He had to do something.

Even if it was only with one foot, Yūichi had stepped into reality, and he couldn't sympathize with the actions of angry teenagers anymore.

Yūichi's figure, sitting on the edge of the bed holding a wet towel to his nose, seemed to have a tired shadow on it. It wasn't just the lack of sleep that caused it: he was losing his youthfulness, and that fatigue was digging roots deep into his young thoughts.

The fact that he had been shunned by the youngsters now demonstrating throughout Herleg sector, and couldn't sympathize with or even understand them, only made it worse.

Yūichi suddenly thought of something, and pinched the muscles of his stomach. They were plenty hard, and resilient—so far. But he somehow couldn't get the same feeling of satisfaction he had felt before, and he felt a kind of irritation.

Yūichi was twenty-three years old: his adolescence had come to an end, although he had been sure it would last forever. He was exactly at the crossroads age, when he had to grasp his life by himself.

From outside came the sound of a caterpillar truck, along with a deep groaning in the ground below, and Yūichi felt the room shake a little.

The police must have called out an armored car to quell the demonstration. Rumor said the ten sleep guns mounted on one armored car had the power to paralyze over two hundred people. After the armored car appeared, there wasn't much hope for the demonstration.

And, in fact, the shouting and screaming grew distant quickly, and finally stopped completely. The window puffed into blackness, and once again the moonlight came gently floating in.

As if it had been hidden, merely waiting for an end to the demonstration's clamor, the refrain of the surf became audible.

Herleg returned, finally, to its usual state of affairs.

2023 :: Age 23

Yūichi let out a yawn, and, rubbing his eyes, was just about to go the bathroom when he heard the sound of breaking glass from the kitchen.

Yūichi was across the room in two short steps, and when he jumped into the kitchen, he hit the lights.

A single youth was crouched in the corner, cowering. He had long hair, and was thin to the point of sickness. There were spatters of blood here and there on his mud-covered shirt. No need to ask: it was clear he was one of the youths who had taken part in the demonstration.

Fear was clearly visible in his eyes, looking up at Yūichi from under the shadow of his long hair. He must have cut himself while breaking the kitchen window: blood was dripping from the back of his hand. Yūichi was frozen, speechless, gripped by some powerful emotion.

He couldn't have been more than six years older than the boy. Even so, that misery-drenched boy quivering in the corner of the kitchen had something Yūichi had lost long ago. Twenty-three was still too young to think about what that might be. He didn't want to think about it.

"What's the matter?" asked Yūichi at last, in a surprisingly relaxed tone. "What do you want?"

"They're chasing me." His voice shook. "Please hide me?"

Just then a violent knock came from the front door. "Police, open up!" It sounded like they were ready to kick the door down.

"Turn off the lights, and stay quiet," said Yūichi, then shut the kitchen door, and turned to the front door without hesitation.

Before he opened the door, he had to even his

breathing a little. The policemen's clamor was certainly directed at the boy, and Yūichi felt bad about subjecting him to their abuses.

When he opened the lock the door groaned as if cracks were running through it, and Yūichi was thrown back, dangerously. With far more force than was called for, the policeman had put his shoulder to the door, and came crashing into the room.

A pair of policemen, wearing typical uniforms. They made the same impression, like two identical twins. A rudely threatening pair, and not nice at all.

"Where is he?"

That was the first thing they said. They seemed to lack the right attitude: to apologize for almost breaking down his door in the middle of the night; for forcing their way into his home. They might have been dressed in uniforms, but they struck him just then as bullies.

Yūichi, slightly amazed, just stood there.

Yūichi had never met such heavy-handed police, especially in Aphrodite. In Yūichi's mind, police helped old people, protected lost children, and so on: the neighborhood cop. On Aphrodite, with its extremely low crime rate, the police had quickly accepted the idea that their work was public service for residents.

And so, when the frequency of the demonstrations began to increase, there was no choice but to bring in more policemen from the outside to bolster the police force. They appeared to be good new officers, but as the number of hires increased, the quality of the police unavoidably fell.

Naturally.

Living in Aphrodite, Yūichi had of course heard

2023 :: Age 23

that sort of rumor occasionally. The *Aphrodite Facsimile* often wrote it up in their articles ... but he had never imagined it might be this bad!

"There's no need to act that scared," said one of the officers as if enjoying it, a thin smile hovering on his lips. "Hand him over nicely, and we won't even mention you."

"I don't know what you're talking about," said Yūichi slowly, after wetting his lips with his tongue. "I want to go back to sleep. If you've got no business, leave, why don't you?"

It was as if he had struck the head of a poisonous snake. As he might have expected, they thrust their heads forward, and bared their fangs.

"Cool it, kid," said one of them, shaking his head and clucking his tongue. "It's *Interference with an Officer in the Performance of his Official Duty*, and that's a bad one, kid."

The other officer loudly snapped open his holster flap, and laid his hand on the butt of his paralysis gun. There was no mistake: if Yūichi showed any resistance at all—like raising his voice—he would pull the trigger of his P-gun without hesitation.

Yūichi wasn't about to become the target of a P-gun.

"No, you two cool it," said Yūichi softly. "This is Mr. Caan's cabin, and I'm his boat boy."

They paled slightly, and stiffened up, standing frozen for a moment and staring at Yūichi. He could see the policeman's trigger finger twitching—a bad sight for the heart.

"OK. We got it," said one of them finally, almost whispering. "Why didn't you say that the in the first place ..."

They left, and Yūichi shut the door. He put his

back against that door for a while, and stood still. The floor under his feet felt even cooler now.

The boy wasn't in the kitchen any longer. When he heard that Yūichi was Mr. Caan's boat boy, he must have flown off again.... Not that Yūichi felt like blaming him for not saying thanks. If he had still been in the kitchen, it would just have meant more trouble for everyone.

That night had been his first really bad experience since coming to Aphrodite; the first really feel-in-the-gut kind of bad. He felt as if someone had smeared mud on the Aphrodite he loved and prized, and that was unbearable.

Yūichi was twenty-three—and his adolescence was coming to an end.

▲

The next morning, Yūichi ran an EV down to the airport to pick up a visitor for Mr. Caan.

Maybe because of lack of sleep, he felt a dull pain deep in his head. On top of the incident of the previous night, Yūichi was in an unusually bad mood.

Yūichi wasn't all that accustomed to being in a bad mood. Basically, he didn't get too upset over things.

It's just the way he was.

He felt his heart rise as he drove from Herleg to Herself, as always. The straight line of his lips broke, naturally, and he felt like humming a tune.

Before he knew it, his headache had vanished entirely.

The sun's radiance poured down and the surface of the six-lane Electronic Control Highway stretching straight ahead, shone white. In sharp contrast to that

2023 :: Age 23

whiteness, the gentle swells of the sea, flashing blue—in fact, he would have been hard pressed to remain melancholy in the midst of this shower of light.

On top of that, today was a special day for Aphrodite. Yūichi owed so much to her, and could not suffer a bad mood on this day of all days. It would be, and no exaggeration, a kind of betrayal.

Today was the twentieth anniversary of the building of Aphrodite. From tonight until tomorrow morning, all of Aphrodite's functions would come to a full stop. The festivities would go on all night, with everyone participating. Everybody was so busy having fun, there was no time to worry about anything—and Yūichi was no exception.

By the time he could see Herself sector, like a cluster of crystals, Yūichi's mood was back to normal.

Mr. Caan's guest was a fat, middle-aged man with a pipe-stem neck and an expression that warned people away.

Yūichi hadn't heard his name, and didn't think he wanted to. Yūichi's job was merely to wait at a certain place at the airport, pick up the guest, and take him to Mr. Caan's house. Anything more than that was unneeded curiosity.

His job was just giving instructions to an electronic control system, but Yūichi was still a living person. It was only reasonable he should have good or bad feelings about people. Even if he didn't say a word, a man he didn't like was still a man he didn't like.

And the man today, he especially didn't like.

He sat in the back seat like a lord, puffing away at a cigar, flicking ashes with total disregard for where they landed. Of course, he didn't say anything, like

"Thank you", to Yūichi—not one word. No doubt it was below his dignity to say anything to the likes of a driver. He was probably some country's politician, and Yūichi felt sympathy for the people in that country—a real unpleasant character.

Yūichi was a boat boy, but sometimes he had to do other tasks as needed. Not just Yūichi: all the boat boys faced the same situation, but it didn't bother him.

Most people thought of "boat boy" as being a vague, part-time kind of thing.

But at times, like today, when he had to pick up nasty people in the EV, he had to think about being twenty-three years old now. *Plus which, this job won't last forever*, he added to himself.

When the car finally reached Mr. Caan's home, it had just turned 9:00 A.M.

After Yūichi had led the guest to the guestroom, he went in search of Mr. Caan.

Mr. Caan was sitting alone, vacantly, in the study.

He was smoking a pipe, and looked as though he was deep in thought. An old wine-jar sat on the desk in front of him.

The door was half-open, but Yūichi hesitated, wondering if it was all right to intrude.

Mr. Caan's figure, backlit by the fire of the morning sun, looked very, very alone. Mr. Caan, who held the glorious throne of the mayor of Aphrodite—the ideal man, the object of every women's dreams—sat dejectedly, with his back bent, like a friendless old man.

It hurt. He felt he had caught a glimpse of an abyss in the man's soul.

Yūichi recalled that he had seen Mr. Caan like this once before. That was years ago, when Mrs.

2023 :: Age 23

Caan had left Aphrodite forever. On that morning, too, Mr. Caan had filled the space around him with the same sense of dejection. And since then, he suddenly realized, Mr. Caan had gotten much older. . . .

Yūichi realized that he, too, had aged by the same amount, and felt an immense sadness.

But he couldn't stand there forever.

"Mr. Caan, . . ." called Yūichi, guardedly. "I've brought your guest."

Mr. Caan turned around with a blank expression. He looked at Yūichi for a time, as if not comprehending what he had said, but at last animation returned.

"Oh . . . Thank you," he said. Then, "Tonight's the Festival. You enjoy yourself, too."

"Yes, sir," Yūichi nodded, and, after a short hesitation, asked "Uh . . . I have a question, sir. . . ."

"Well, what?" Mr. Caan took the pipe from his lips and looked at Yūichi.

"Did you know there was a youth demonstration last night?"

"Mm . . . Thanks to it, I got no sleep, and have no idea of what to do about it."

"It . . . Before, I borrowed the *Rosebud* without permission, and had an accident. You remember, sir?"

The other nodded, remaining silent.

"You said then, that for the city of Aphrodite to be energetic, Aphrodite needed impulsive youth. . . . Are you thinking of the kids who took part in that demonstration in the same way? Can you really file the problem away like that?"

Yūichi had no idea himself why he asked such a question—his question, and the memory of Mr. Caan's words, had occurred to him in an instant.

Still, even though he didn't know why, he couldn't stop, and he seemed to have asked the question without really meaning to.

Mr. Caan put the pipe in his mouth again. He seemed to be drawing heavily, but there was no sign of flame, only the wet sound of air being sucked through the pipe.

"Damn . . . I've wet it again. . . ." he muttered quietly, and then turned to Yūichi and asked "Do you have any idea when this wine jar was made?"

"No." Yūichi shook his head, dazed. He had absolutely no idea why Mr. Caan would suddenly start in about the wine jar.

"It was excavated on Crete, in the ruins of Knossos. It's a beautiful jar, isn't it? I almost can't believe that a civilization capable of producing such a beautiful jar existed before Christ. . . ."

Mr. Caan cut his words there, and said in an almost derisive voice, ". . . and even that Cretan civilization perished, vanished completely . . ."

After Mr. Caan rose, and left to go to the living room, Yūichi thought for a while about what the words meant.

He had absolutely no idea.

2

The city seemed to be in a good mood, bustling as it waited for the night's festival to start.

Even the usually prim Herself sector, girded in inorganic armor, today was overflowing of gaiety and excitement, as if it had awakened and were smiling.

Part of it was due to the throngs of tourists from overseas, come to see the sights of the Twentieth Anniversary Festival. According to the Bureau of Tourism, the number of tourists on Aphrodite today was over three times more than usual.

And that was a lot. The tourists—the men dressed in polo shirts, and the women in tank tops— paraded through the streets in their light clothes, shouting at everything: a constant hum of voices laughing together.

The cheerful voice of the Aphrodite Kid came pouring out from all over. Here and there, in the plazas, the free champagne and beer sponsored by Aphrodite City overflowed, and the merry tourists danced their ring ever larger. There was laughter, the sound of popping popcorn, and the fragrant smell of frying hamburgers.

Ice cream and soft drinks were handed out for the kids as they hung on the counters, their voices piping shrilly.

Aphrodite

"Come on, come on, line up . . . Nothing for children with bad manners!" called the huge ice-cream man in a white apron, as he shook his protruding belly with laughter.

More balloons than could possibly be counted floated in the sky. Silver balloons blindingly reflected the sun, and even the non-silvered ones filled the crystal-clear air of Aphrodite with light.

In one of the plazas, a famous circus flown in from Germany had set up a scarlet, one-ring tent. The acrobats had sallied forth into the street, and the brave sound of cymbals rang out. They were flipping and somersaulting to all.

The Festival.

It was Aphrodite's festival.

All of Aphrodite's boats and ships were in the harbor, from sailboats to junks, painting the radiance of the bay in color. When night fell, their decorative lights flickered, forming ever-changing patterns of light.

The smell of ozone, the roar of the waves, the flashing sun of the South Seas . . . Today, Aphrodite was more beautiful than ever. The clear, rich, complaint-free taste of the perfect wine.

Between the sea and the impossibly clear sky towered clouds, rolled up together.

Their pure white radiance celebrated Aphrodite, smiling together with her.

There was even a rainbow.

People stirred together, and looked at the sky. A giant, brilliant rainbow showed its perfect form, rising into the sky, as real and solid as if it had concentrated all the day's sunlight into a single arch. It was a rainbow you might see only once or twice in a lifetime. . . .

2023 :: Age 23

The rainbow had been planned by the Aphrodite Anniversary Festival Committee, and their success in weather control and spectrum art was drawn on the sky for all to see. It announced that now the real festival would begin: a kind of "go" sign.

From now until the middle of the night, it was Festival time, and the fever would rise, and rise.

▲

Yūichi had promised to meet Gil and Voight at the Laugh Cat.

There was still some time until then, though, and he figured it would be better to eat lunch first.

The number of times Yūichi had eaten in Herself sector could be counted on one hand. Whatever else it may have been, Herself sector was the center of Aphrodite, and the restaurant prices there were a bit too steep for most young people.

Still, today was a special day: it was the Festival. Yūichi figured there couldn't be anything wrong with allowing himself the luxury of eating at a high-class restaurant today.

The fact was, Yūichi had been searching for an excuse to eat at a certain restaurant.

The restaurant, serving Italian food, was built on top of one of the free-floating foundations that supported Aphrodite. All four walls were made of pressure-resistant glass: it was one of the so-called "in-the-ocean" restaurants that let customers watch the marine life while eating.

Actually, it wasn't at all a high-class restaurant, but rather aimed straight at the masses. Just being located in Herself sector was enough to make Yūichi think of it as a high-class place.

Aphrodite

The restaurant was almost full.

Most of the customers seemed to be tourists. An excited, laughing voice carried from one of the tables. No doubt someone was already drunk.

After Yūichi smoothed his hair down, and tucked the hem of his shirt into his pants, he puffed out his chest a little, and entered the restaurant with long strides.

He took a seat all the way in the back, and looked around, absorbing what were, for him, unusual surroundings. He felt he had come to a terribly wrong place; but at the same time he also felt that he had somehow suddenly become the center of everyone's attention—that kind of pride.

For Yūichi, born in a solidly middle-class home in Tokyo, and who had been eating at the Laugh Cat since he first came to Aphrodite, it was only natural that this underwater restaurant should seem gorgeous.

It wasn't, though, not really; merely unique.

Countless schools of fish crossed before the pressure glass, exhaling silver bubbles. The bubbles painted the restaurant in blue—floating in the midst of ever-moving shadows. It was certainly not a small restaurant, but it felt small, like a fishbowl.

So: it was unique. For exactly that reason tourists came here, gathered here, and loved it.

After he finished ordering, and was just beginning to feel at peace, a conspicuously loud voice came from the table to his side—overbearing and obviously not caring that he bothered other diners.

The braying laugh belonged to a middle-aged man, apparently a tourist, wearing dark sunglasses. He was engrossed in his conversation, waving his fork in his hand. His listener was a youngish man,

2023 :: Age 23

with a slight smile playing as if he had been shut up, making vague affirmative sounds as he listened.

At once, Yūichi recalled the middle-aged fat man he had met at the airport that morning. They certainly looked to have the same common imprint of self-importance.

"I mean, really . . . Caan is just too clever, don't you think?" The man in sunglasses gave a big laugh. "Still, no matter how clever you are, there are still things that are possible and there are things that aren't. Mm? Right? Right!" It seemed that Mr. Caan had become the topic of their conversation. Yūichi found himself listening to their words.

The man's young companion said something in a small voice, and as if to drown him out, the man in sunglasses spoke in a deep voice. "Well, right? Certainly, Aphrodite is a handy thing for development of ocean resources, but hell, it still depends on the major nations, doesn't it? It's a little hard to swallow them saying that they want to protect their character as a semi-independent state while doing favors for the major powers."

The younger tried to interject something, but the man in sunglasses raised his hand, cutting him off, and began to expound.

"I know, I know. You want to say that Caan's ideal is the city-state, right? I think that's just a pile of dreck. . . . Anyway, listen . . . The whole darn world is turning into a mental ward. Or a junkyard. In this oh-so-wonderful world, no nation is doing all that great. Anywhere. So why is only Aphrodite doing well? Why is only Aphrodite so special?" He stopped there for a minute, then continued with even more venom.

"Because it's living off other countries. Because

it's living off us! That's why I say Caan is too clever. It doesn't stand to reason that Aphrodite will stay this way forever. Do you know that America and Canada are working on a floating ocean resource development factory? When that's completed, Aphrodite's development efficiency won't even compare. There's the same rumor coming out of Russia ... No doubt about it: Aphrodite will collapse. It'll become the same as the other countries, a mental ward and junk heap. And not in the distant future, either."

"Shut up!" The shout burst out, piercing through Yūichi's throat. His head was suddenly hot, and his self-control gone. He didn't even notice himself standing up.

At Yūichi's outburst, the restaurant became deathly silent, everyone staring. Above the heads of the customers with vacantly gaping mouths, the shadows of grazing fish slowly passed the pressure glass.

"Please, stop it?" asked Yūichi in a completely different voice, weakly talking, almost to himself. "Please, stop?"

The man in sunglasses was frozen speechless. At last, he muttered deep in his throat.

"What's he so upset about?" Then he turned to his young companion, and repeated it. "What is this young fool all upset about?"

"I'm telling you not to insult Aphrodite!" said Yūichi, waving his hands. "And I won't let you insult Mr. Caan, either."

"Jeez! Where did this guy come from?" spat out the man in sunglasses, rolling his eyes.

"Excuse me ..." said the younger man, coolly. "It's really none of your business what we talk about, is it?"

"If you're going to insult Aphrodite, get out of this

2023 :: Age 23

city. And don't insult Mr. Caan, either, because you don't have the vaguest idea what kind of man he is!" As Yūichi began to clamor again, a hand grabbed his shoulder from behind. When he turned, there was the angry face of the manager.

"The person that's leaving is you," said the manager, roughly. "You're gonna stop picking quarrels with other customers."

". . ."

Yūichi realized the fault was his, and stood rooted in blank amazement.

The anger seething in him began to fade rapidly—it was true: it was none of his business what other people talked about. Even accused of picking fights, he couldn't say a word.

"I'm sorry. . . ." Yūichi submitted his apology in a mutter. As Yūichi despondently left the restaurant, the man in sunglasses heaped scorn on his disgrace.

"Not only is Aphrodite willfully self-indulgent, but so are the punks who live here!"

Not even one word.

Yūichi's indignation had gone too far, and he had to admit it was pretty unusual for him to blow up like that in front of people he didn't even know.

Yūichi understood what had happened—the man in the sunglasses was only a trigger. Yūichi had been wired like a tomcat in a bad mood, an explosion just waiting to go off.

Why?

To Yūichi, Aphrodite was everything. Only this city gave him the vibrant breath of life, and brought him satisfaction. He couldn't survive anywhere else.

To Yūichi, Aphrodite was something to believe in.

He felt that the winds of change had begun to

blow in Aphrodite, though it should have been perfect. He couldn't put his finger on it, but something had begun to fade, something that made him feel the vitality was ebbing.

The frequency of the demonstrations, the quality of the hired police ... These were superficial, mere phenomena. He felt a foreboding that something essential, the heart that made Aphrodite *Aphrodite* was breaking down. Like a house with termites eating away at the foundations, it was clear that Aphrodite, too, would collapse.

Of course it was nothing more than a vaguely felt premonition, with nothing he could really point a finger at. Maybe it was just because he had gotten older, and could no longer enjoy the pleasures of Aphrodite as innocently as before.

Still, as Yūichi began to walk towards the Ocean Promenade, Mr. Caan's words echoed insistently in his head, obstinately refusing to disappear.

And even that Cretan civilization perished, vanished completely....

Even so, that vague melancholy vanished completely from Yūichi's heart the second he set foot in Herhip sector.

Herhip, too, was bursting with the gaiety of the Festival! The Festival! The refined atmosphere of Herself was gone: no pretense or pose, just the energy of people enjoying the Festival to the fullest, like it was bubbling up from the streets.

With brave bangs, firecrackers were spitting flame and skittering along the flagstones. Confetti was dancing in the air, and a fiddle melody echoed. Men and women both were possessed by dance, and the sound of clapping surged like a tsunami.

2023 :: Age 23

The gorgeous, multicolored clothing of the dancers flooded the streets . . .

It was a mix of many ethnic festivals, nothing more than slightly bad taste—to be blunt: nothing but a farce, a wild spree. Still, if the goal of a festival was to free people from the yoke of their ordinary lives, then these crowds clearly knew how to enjoy it.

Maybe the prim flavor of the Twentieth Anniversary Festival remained in Herself sector; but here, people were enjoying the Festival for its own sake. This energy that shattered the day's gentleness in one smash was the underlying power of Herhip itself.

He had a tough time of it before he finally arrived at the Laugh Cat. People insisted he drink their beer, or women embraced him, and he had to stop time and time again.

To be honest, by the time Yūichi arrived at the Laugh Cat, he was totally worn out and not a little drunk.

"Hey, you made it!" bellowed Tarloff, standing on the counter pinning decorations to the ceiling. "It must be a madhouse outside."

Yūichi, without answering, slumped down in a chair at one of the round tables for the time being. His cheeks were hot, and his chest throbbed.

Sue, who was cleaning behind the counter, tipped a little water into a glass, and brought it to him. Yūichi drank it in one gulp, and after letting out a big sigh, greeted Sue. "Thanks."

Sue smiled at him. For just that one instant her constant look of sadness was gone, revealing the lovely expression of a young woman. Yūichi, blankly, realized he knew practically nothing at all about her. Considering he'd met her over five years ago, that was a little unnatural.

But Sue, avoiding involvement as always, slipped back behind the counter after taking the glass from Yūichi's hand. She was used to being ignored.

"So you finally came." Gil came out of the back, carrying a bouquet of string lights. His long, horse-like face was red with alcohol, and looked pretty funny. Maybe if you held a carrot in front of a horse, it might have that kind of laughing face.

After their submersible race five years before, Gil had been fired as a boat boy, and had managed to get a job at a small travel agency. What the people around him—and he himself—couldn't believe was that he had been working seriously since. It seemed he had a talent for sales, and his performance wasn't bad at all.

Yūichi, together with Gil, got up on the table, and began to string the ceiling with glass-fiber illumination.

Once it got dark there was sure to be a flood of people streaming from the Festival to the Laugh Cat. They had to finish hanging the decorations in time.

"Did you hear about Anita?" asked Gil, while stringing illumination from the ceiling.

"Uh-huh," nodded Yūichi. "If you mean that she was selected as a runner-up for the Aphrodite 'Aphrodite', I heard."

"Not just an ordinary runner-up. She's in the finals."

"Huh?"

"For real."

"That's fantastic!"

"Well, they'll have the finals tonight. She might become the Aphrodite 'Aphrodite'!"

2023 :: Age 23

"Fantastic!" repeated Yūichi.

The Aphrodite "Aphrodite" was one of the entertainments of the Twentieth Anniversary Festival, aiming to select the most beautiful woman of all. The first round was an open selection, with hundreds of candidates, and after a vote by the citizens of Aphrodite to order the group, Anita had been one of the finalists. And, he had to admit, that was indeed fantastic.

When the conversation turned to Anita, Gil and Yūichi both acted as if it were a ticklish topic, treading tenderly. They still remembered their race five years ago, when they were deciding who would have first date with Anita, and they felt a kind of embarrassed memory at it. Then, they had been eighteen, and Anita only sixteen....

"Aah, the entrance of the Aphrodite 'Aphrodite'?!" bellowed Tarloff in his bold voice.

"Hi!" Anita greeted everyone with a smile as she entered the Laugh Cat.

Beautiful... even looking at her as Voight's wife, Yūichi couldn't help but recall what he had felt the first time they had met. He couldn't help but be a little envious of Voight's happiness. It was always that way.

Of course, Anita wasn't a girl any more. The vivid impression she had had when they first met had withdrawn, and in its place was a graceful, relaxed beauty. She had been married to Voight for over a year now, so maybe that was only natural... Maybe Anita's really beautiful period was just starting.

"We heard about it," called Gil. "A finalist for the Aphrodite 'Aphrodite'! That's great! You might be named *The Most Beautiful Woman in Aphrodite!*"

"Oh, be quiet... I won't be able to show my face in public if I lose!" smiled Anita as Voight appeared behind her. He waved a hand in a casual greeting to everyone, then wrapped his arm around Anita's shoulder, and they entered together. They were a well-matched couple.

Every time he saw Voight, Yūichi felt a little awed. Not from a complex, but because he felt from his heart that he and Voight were made differently. Voight had always been a relaxed, trustworthy person, but since he had been trusted with the management of the *Aphrodite Facsimile*, he had somehow grown even more so. It was only natural he had fallen in love with Anita.

After he separated from Anita, he came straight to Yūichi and said in a low voice, almost a whisper, "I've got something I need to talk to you about . . . Can we talk alone for a minute?"

"Something to tell me? What?"

"About your employer," said Voight quietly. "I've got something about Mr. Caan that I want you to hear. . . ."

3

The doves were freed, released to the sky.

They fluttered up in a cloudburst, blocking the sun's light for an instant, making the interior of the room flicker like a broken light. He could hear shouting, the hum of laughing voices. He heard the crash of cymbals, the reverberations continuing for a time, and then everyone fell quet.

The voice of the Aphrodite Kid was audible from somewhere. He was pleading that if he only had love, he didn't need anything else. Only a single dove was left roosting on the stucco outside the window. It cooed, and after cocking its head a little, cooed again. It seemed to be at a loss.

"Wish I'd brought some peanuts or something . . . I could have given some to the doves," said Yūichi, then returned his attention to Voight, and asked "What do you need to talk to me about?"

"Mm . . ." Voight nodded, and stared at the table for a time. He wasn't the usual cool Voight, but seemed to be wondering how to phrase his words.

They were in a room on the second floor of the Laugh Cat. It was quiet there, away from the commotion of the streets.

"I wanted to ask you, . . ." Voight finally said. "This morning, you took a visitor from the airport to Mr. Caan's home."

"Uh-huh...." Yūichi frowned. "Why do you know that?"

"Was he the man in this photograph?" Without answering Yūichi's question, Voight took a single photo from his pants pocket, and placed it on the table: it was a picture of a middle-aged man with a pipe-stem neck, looking bad-tempered, puffing on a cigar. No doubt about it, it was the man from that morning.

"Yeah, that's him ... but ..."

"He works for the Defense Services Assistance Agency, the DSAA. He's a military man from the Pentagon," said Voight rapidly, cutting him off. "Why did Mr. Caan have to meet this man? That's what I want to know."

"..." Yūichi stared fixedly at Voight's face.

"I want to know very badly," repeated Voight, and then looked directly into Yūichi's face. "I have to know."

"So what are you saying I should do?"

"I want you to find out for me."

"You're saying I should be a spy?"

"If you want to use that word, yeah, I guess so."

"No!" Yūichi spat out from between clenched teeth. "I refuse."

The feeling that a wind of change was sweeping through Aphrodite, something strange, returned to him even stronger than before, grabbing, squeezing his chest. And now it was blowing between him and his closest friends. Was he sad? Of course he was sad. More than the sadness, though, was the emptiness he felt.

"I respect Mr. Caan," said Yūichi. "It would be impossible for me to spy on Mr. Caan, impossible."

"Me, too. As an individual, I like Mr. Caan, I respect him. But he's the mayor of Aphrodite. If Mr.

2023 :: Age 23

Caan, the mayor, is trying to arrange something with a man from the DSAA, I, as a journalist, have to find out the truth...."

Voight said that much in a single breath, as if possessed, then suddenly snapped his mouth shut, turning his head away. "Never mind. Forget I asked."

"Voight..."

"Please, you never heard anything."

"..."

"Uh..."

"Promise?"

"I never heard a thing," nodded Yūichi.

They both fell silent, unable to continue. They had nothing they needed to say. It was a terrible, hurt silence—Yūichi felt Voight had receded, had become a total stranger. Maybe it wasn't entirely an illusion.

Just then, a knock sounded, and Gil's voice broke in. "Hey, we're going soon."

They both stood up quickly, saved by the voice. When they left the room, they yielded to each other at the door like strangers.

▲

It was well known that Mr. Caan had begun construction of Aphrodite with the ideal of the ancient Greek city-state in mind. They said that the image he really had in mind was a temple to Poseidon—the one that was still standing near Athens on Cape Sounion—or the Temple of Athena. There was little doubt that those two temples, built long before Christ, still cast a great influence over Aphrodite.

When those temples built on that Sounion Cape,

that yearned toward the Aegean Sea, flashed pure white in the sun, or when they were painted deep red in the evening glow, they shared something with Aphrodite.

In a city-state—for example, in ancient Athens—a plaza was essential: a place to discuss, to converse, to gather together freely. A plaza was conceived as being at the core all civic life.

For the city-state, a plaza for the citizens was a symbol of freedom and wisdom.

Naturally, when Mr. Caan designed Aphrodite he was strongly conscious of this function of the plaza within the city-state. He had delved deeply into this concept—one might call it the "plaza ideal"—enlarging and reinterpreting it.

Mr. Caan took the plaza to be, first of all, a public space. To him, that made it a place where people could refresh themselves, partake of easy conversation, work together; in other words, a space that was free of all restrictions.

It was a re-creation of the local playground where children went, liberated by sheer freedom to achieve a magical commonality, a sense of community, but on a scale hundreds of times larger.

Was that really possible?

It was easy to say "Return to the innocence of a child," but was it really possible for adults who had traveled their own meandering paths through life to return to the playgrounds of childhood just by giving them a plaza?

Mr. Caan's ideas were regarded as the ultimate in desktop academic theories. Many leading architects looked down their noses, and dismissed the plaza as merely another piece of refuse added to the huge mountain of junk that was Aphrodite.

2023 :: Age 23

Still, Mr. Caan had—up to a certain point—succeeded in reviving the playground in people's hearts with Cestus Square.

The Cestus was the embroidered belt of the goddess Aphrodite, said to arouse the power of love, and Cestus Square was located in the center of Herself sector.

It had to fulfill two contradictory functions: it had to be widely open to the public, to the outside; but it also had to make the people who gathered there aware of that sense of "community."

It was impossible for Cestus Square to be indoors. At the same time—to foster a shared awareness—it couldn't be a totally open space, either. As a result, it was festooned with canopies that could be opened or closed freely, like the petals of the lotus blossom.

Except for special circumstances, the canopies were not opened or closed manually, but instead run by a weather-based controller. The wind always blew there, the radiance of the sun drenched the earth, and the tang of the sea was ever present: sensitive to weather changes, the computer opened or closed the lotuses incrementally in response.

There were no walls in Cestus. Not even any fences. Herself sector was totally open here: an absurdly huge open space. Cestus Square was, however, full of giant columns, each so thick that two people would have had difficulty encircling one with their arms. They were in the Greek Doric style, with vertical grooves carved into them, but were not there to support the canopies. The lotus canopies, which opened and closed magnetically, needed no physical support: when the lotus flowers were open, the columns climbed up into the blue sky. Truly, it was a view that recalled the ruins of the temple on Cape Sounion.

At first glance it looked as if the columns were placed at random, but in fact they were carefully positioned for psychological effect. If you chose any three, or four, or five, columns—however many you liked—suddenly, a virtual "enclosed space" would become a reality. People could, in response to their need, voluntarily create a closed space within the limitless open space around them.

Cestus Square was open. Still, if you wanted to, you could gather your friends together in the enclosed spaces created by the columns, and could affirm that warmth of friendship together. For groups that desired even more isolation, the columns could generate semi-transparent air curtains that would block noise and prying eyes. The pale purple or yellow air curtains were beautiful, enthralling.

Cestus Square, open wide to the outer world, and allowing the people that gathered there to reaffirm their group identity, was indeed a rare type of public space.

Mr. Caan's genius as an architect had been up to the challenge from the start.

The lotus blossom canopies of Cestus Square were always moving as if rustling in the wind. With three-, four- and five-column realms wrapped in pale mist scattered here and there throughout the plaza, it floated like a dream. Glittering light—probably from the solar cells—ran flashing like crystallized sunbeams along the grooves carved in the columns, which were surrounded by masses of greenery, with countless flowers in bloom.

As the plaza symbolized the city-state, so you

2023 :: Age 23

could say that Cestus Square symbolized Aphrodite.

The announcement of this year's Aphrodite "Aphrodite" would be made in a corner of Cestus Square.

▲

Dusk was approaching.

As the indigo sky began to deepen, the earth grew brighter in contrast. Just as black game pieces are flipped over to reveal their red backs, so was Aphrodite adorned with illuminated beads, draped and decorated.

The brilliant—but still strangely transparent—light of Aphrodite blended into the saffron atmosphere, and sparkled at random off the incoming wave crests.

You could hear the voice of the Aphrodite Kid faintly. The Kid's voice was almost lost in the roar of the surf, but never quite vanished completely, echoing through Cestus Square.

Aphrodite's Twentieth Anniversary Festival was finally about to be unveiled.

The Kid's voice, booming from the speakers, was at full volume, but there was no distortion. It flowed perfectly, smoothly to their ears: the columns of Cestus Square had been built with an eye towards acoustic fidelity.

The stage for the Aphrodite "Aphrodite" took up about half of Cestus Square. Almost ten thousand people were gathered there, eating and drinking the prepared refreshments—free!—and waiting for the announcement of the winner.

It was splendid, gorgeous.

The air curtain shined like agate, wrapping the stage in a liquid waterfall of light. Crimson, flaring letters spelling out "Aphrodite" floated back and forth over the crowd. Along with the Kid's voice, the complicated mesh of the lasers over the stage formed a shape like a cat's cradle.

In the center of Cestus Square was a giant pool. From the lights at the bottom of the pool, pillars of water-clear blue light rose almost to the tops of the lotus blossoms, as if piercing the Square with icicles. In those pillars of light, perhaps through some advanced optical technology, the shapes of swimmers were clearly reflected. Bypassing the law of gravity, their shapes floated up and down the pillars of light.

Countless tiny single-seat blimps were floating above the crowd. If you whistled, the responder would activate, and the blimp would slowly descend. You straddled it, found your balance with your body, and went where you wanted without bumping elbows.

The semi-transparent blouses of the girls, the fragrant smell of the bubbly drinks, the sparkling of the fountains, laughter, the scattered flowers, the murmurs of love . . .

It was like a dream. No, it *was* a dream. No mistake, this was a dream.

While Yūichi was prowling for food and drink, he strayed from Gil and Voight. He suddenly noticed that only Anita was left by his side.

"What'll we do?" asked Yūichi, scratching his head for something to say. "We'd better find them again."

"It's OK," said Anita, relaxed. "It'd be much more

2023 :: Age 23

clever to wait here for them to find us." At the word "us," spoken in that matter-of-fact tone, Yūichi lost his composure a little. There were some things that people just couldn't get used to. For Yūichi, it was being alone with Anita.

After being selected as a finalist for the Aphrodite "Aphrodite," Anita's beauty had taken another quantum leap beyond the rest. She shone.

Like all beautiful women, Anita walked with perfect composure, confident the world would open a path for her. And the world always did. Yūichi admired her splendid figure as she walked some paces ahead of him, and watched her. He still couldn't get used to her beauty.

Suddenly the agate-colored radiance of the air-curtains turned black, and at the same time the background music of the Kid broke off. The pillars of light from the pool vanished, and even the blimps stopped as if frozen in space—people's voices became lower, then quiet, and at last the area was completely silent.

In the darkened, twilit area, only the flaming letters "Aphrodite" floated clearly.

"We now announce the lucky winner of the crown and the glory of the Aphrodite's 'Aphrodite,'" echoed a rich baritone voice.

"And the winner is . . . this Goddess!"

Some distance from the lotus blossoms, an orange light switched on. Like the plasma rockets that cut through space, it cut through the gray darkness and came to rest at one woman's feet. At Anita's feet.

"You won!" A shout of joy burst from Yūichi's throat. There was a pause for an instant, then the area burst into clamor, and the sound of applause cascaded down onto Anita—and, as if Anita was dizzy too, she held her hands to her cheeks, and stood rooted to the spot. The lights exploded. A torrent of blinding radiance ran between the people like fireworks, exploding. A spray of light came pouring down. The air curtains released crimson glitter and slowly undulated, painting the stage in all the colors of the rainbow—and the flaming letters spelling "A-p-h-r-o-d-i-t-e" flashed as if shaking with laughter.

The Kid's song *Praise for Aphrodite* was playing quietly and the lotus blossom canopies began to open slowly. Blue-tinted columns of fire rose from the pool in a straight line, up between the opened canopies; columns of radiance rose toward the starry sky, climbing, climbing... Maybe all the way to the stars.

Anita had recovered from her excitement, and was standing elegantly in the light, beaming with joy: her usual smile. In response to the applause, she waved her hands slightly.

A silver blimp came gliding into the area, and began to drop slowly after coming to a stop above Anita. It resembled a horse who had seen its master, and was trotting to greet her.

The noise from the stage grew even greater, and the sounds of "bravo" and applause continued for some time.

Anita glanced at Yūichi over her shoulder, and laughed in a clear voice. Then she sat lightly on the blimp, sidesaddle, and snapped the seat belt shut.

It rose gently, and began to move slowly over the crowd. Anita's waving figure was elegant, refined, and like a queen. Her beauty befit Aphrodite's "Aphrodite."

Yūichi was lost in applauding. He was full of a kind

2023 :: Age 23

of pride that made him want to boastfully walk in front of everyone—although, rationally, Yūichi had neither the need nor the qualifications to do so.

The din of shouts and applause continued until her blimp rose beyond the open lotus blossoms, and vanished.

For a while waves of excitement swept the area. High, laughing voices could be heard indistinctly, and comments praising Anita's beauty were heard here and there.

Still, even that commotion began to die down after a while, and the crowd began to thin before his eyes. Once the Aphrodite "Aphrodite" was chosen, there was no need to stay here any more.

People shifted their interest from Anita herself to considering how the Anniversary Committee was planning to use her in the festivities. Yūichi, planning to go out on the town together with Gil and Voight, started walking around Cestus Square, looking for them. The air curtains were no longer stretched between the columns, and the robots were rapidly but jerkily cleaning up the area, moving like an old movie.

When Cestus Square transformed again to an open space, the people who had looked so crowded before now looked very sparse, even lonely.

Colored illumination, and the sight of the little circus pushing its triangular tents into that sea of light, peeped between the columns from the direction of Herhip sector.

When he reached the edge of Cestus Square, Yūichi felt something, someone's shoulder, hit him in the back. When he turned to look, there was the face of the boy who had fled his kitchen that morning.

"Huh? You?" smiled Yūichi, but quickly wiped off his smile.

The boy wasn't smiling, but rather a faintly hostile expression hovered on his hard, stubborn face. He wasn't alone: another four boys stood behind him like a gang.

"There's something I want from you," said the boy, like beating a drum.

"Like what?" Yūichi lowered his eyebrows.

"You, you work as a boat boy for Caan, you said . . . I want you to meet us sometimes, and tell us anything you can about him."

". . ." Yūichi, astonished, stared into the boy's face. Part of it was the boy's audacity, just going too far; and the other part was how much it resembled what Voight had asked—it left him momentarily speechless.

"It's useless," said one of the boys, looking away. "He works for Caan. No way he's got any balls."

"Yeah, I guess you're right," nodded the boy in front of Yūichi, and turned to face the others. "Let's go."

They had turned on their heels, and were beginning to slump away, when the anger finally came boiling up into Yūichi's heart. It wasn't just anger towards the boys. Better to say that the indignation, the frustration, he felt towards whatever it was that was fracturing Aphrodite, towards the thing that was casting Mr. Caan as an evil man, had finally appeared. Here.

"Wait." At his pointed voice, they stopped, and slowly turned around.

"What?" sneered one of them.

"Apologize! Apologize for bad-mouthing Mr. Caan and me."

2023 :: Age 23

The boys looked at each other, bewildered. Then one of the boys in the middle spoke, in an unexpectedly calm voice.

"We admit we were rude. When we heard you were worked for Mr. Caan, we got a little tense.... So we apologize for saying that about you ... But we won't apologize for Mr. Caan. That goes against our principles."

"Apologize!" Yūichi cut through his words. The unpleasant silence hung there for a while.

"Do you have any idea?" asked another boy at last, disgustedly. "Do you understand where Aphrodite is now? Sure, it's gone well up to now. Whatever else it might be, Aphrodite is the only floating city, and they need it to exploit ocean resources. But now all the big countries are building floating factory cities. Aphrodite is about to lose her biggest asset, the only valuable part of her existence. At worst, she might lose her status as a semi-independent nation.... And if that happens it would be very, very bad to have Caan as mayor, because he thinks Aphrodite is his private property. Do you know his reputation as a manipulator? To remain mayor, Caan could easily sell Aphrodite out to the major powers...."

"Apologize," repeated Yūichi.

"Let's go." Another boy, who had been silent until then, shook his head. "It's no use talking to this guy."

As they turned and started to go for the second time, Yūichi suddenly bent down, and ran full force into the middle of the group, head-first.

"Uh ..." The boy who had taken Yūichi's head full in the stomach fell to the ground, coughing.

"What the hell?"

While they were still trying to figure out what

had happened, Yūichi punched another boy on the jaw. He tottered backwards, and collapsed to sit vacantly on the pavement.

The anger that had been building up inside Yūichi came exploding out, exploding him. He waved his arms wildly, without caring who he hit, trying to kick whoever he could. He knew he had been hit a number of times, but his excitement was so high he couldn't feel the pain. Unfortunately, though, Yūichi wasn't used to fighting, and his punches were not all that strong. When he punched somebody, they hurt; but a five-to-one fight was not one he could win.

Yūichi finally had his arms grabbed from behind, and was repeatedly beaten with what felt like a sandbag. He tried to free his arms somehow, or to twist his body; but couldn't get the leverage from that unnatural position.

A fist came striking at his eyes, and as a reflex he jerked his head away, taking an explosive hit on the temple. He felt himself go foggy, and the power drained from his knees. He knew, with a strange clarity, that if he were hit again, he would lose consciousness.

Suddenly, his body was free.

He collapsed onto the street, falling over untidily. He was busy catching his breath for a while. With the blood pounding through his temples, it was hard to concentrate on anything.

After a minute or two, he noticed that the boys were busy fighting someone other than himself.

He made a huge effort, and finally raised his head up. He stared dizzily at the human figures in motion around him, and tried to focus on them. The figures were mixed together, and constantly changing position, so he couldn't quite made out the faces clearly.

2023 :: Age 23

He saw Gil's face.

Then he saw Voight's face.

They were fighting well, but they hadn't quite mastered the boys. Gil was doing OK, but Voight wasn't used to fighting, and was barely managing to put in a blow for every two he received. He was, bluntly, too clumsy.

Seeing Voight, who was always cool and calm, fighting with his cheeks puffed out, Yūichi felt his chest tighten with a flame of emotion.

The unspoken tension between himself and Voight vanished like it had never existed. The fellowship they had enjoyed as teenagers came flashing back—Yūichi, now, could enjoy the Festival from the bottom of his heart.

Yūichi gathered the shout of gladness rising from his heart into his body, and managed to stand. Then he gave a laugh, and started to jump into the fray.

"Idiot!" Gil grabbed Yūichi from behind. "Come on!" The three of them, Yūichi, Gil and Voight, fled together.

While they were running, all three of them were laughing.

▲▲▲▲ 4

Night.

Aphrodite gradually lost its glitter, like a single huge gem, turning to somber shadows.

It was still the Festival, but there was no longer any resplendence here, just the usual lights of the town.

In contrast to Aphrodite's fading, the sea shining in the moonlight was now clearly visible. The waves came rolling in; the light a pale glitter on the tide as it beat peacefully against the shore—there was even the blue glow of plankton floating among the waves.

What had happened to Aphrodite?

Now, when it should be playing, he couldn't hear the voice of the Aphrodite Kid. Aphrodite was totally silent, as if it were holding its breath, an almost unpleasant silence.

The sound of the wind, the roar of the tide . . . But nothing happened.

Aphrodite seemed to be squatting in the darkness.

Still, something was slowly, quietly—but definitely—signaling a change.

For example, the sound of the waves.

The refrain of the waves, which had been regular until now, had pauses and irregularities. Without listening closely, it was very hard to hear the change, but unquestionably the waves were crashing together as if there were a sudden gust on the sea. The sounds of waves crashing, and falling in disarray could be heard.

The sound of the waves grew more and more irregular, and finally showed a clear, unmistakable *difference*.

A heavy echo began to resound, and at the same time a bright light lit up the area from below the surface of the sea.

Like wildfire on a deserted plain, the radiance came rushing over the ocean, following the wave dampers to envelope Aphrodite in a wall of ocean.

The sea level rose ten meters, then fell like a waterfall, throwing off a huge spray.

The spray floated like steam, and each drop, burning with that terrible light, shone like a pearl.

From the bubbling, frothing sea surface, you could see that compressed gases were escaping . . . Clearly an artificial phenomenon.

The pale silhouette of Aphrodite was surrounded by the blue wall of the sea, a phantasm. Countless tons of water fell in a cacophony of echoes, but even so the atmosphere was peaceful, tranquil, thanks to the blue light shining from the bottom of the sea, enveloping Aphrodite gently. It was a pale, soft light; but yet mysteriously tenacious.

Suddenly, the light crystallized, seemed to take human form. Slowly, a human figure rose.

It was Anita.

No, Anita was Aphrodite.

Just as the Renaissance artists had painted, she was born from a bed of sea foam, standing elegantly on a shell: the second coming of Aphrodite.

Anita had only a thin cloth wrapped around

2023 :: Age 23

her, leaving her figure close to nude. But none of the watchers felt lust at her glowing, perfectly white breasts, or her soft shoulders, or her straight legs. At least, not in Aphrodite city—no one.

With her naked body, she had transcended sex, bathing them in an emotion beyond sex. It wasn't the special sensuality of her beauty, but the symbolism—she was beauty embodied.

The goddess Aphrodite of myth had returned to the world, the Goddess of Beauty.

Her pure beauty, and the skill of holographic art advanced almost to perfection, made the miracle possible.

Anita was enlarged, made gigantic, but she still had that playful smile, her hair was waving slightly in the wind, and she had the delicate beauty to perfectly match the myth.

Anita was Aphrodite.

Born from the sea foam, she was a new Aphrodite symbolizing Aphrodite's freedom, love, glory, naiveté, naturalness... All the good things. It wasn't just because the Anniversary Committee chose her to be Aphrodite: it was also because she was perfect for the role.

When Anita's hologram came to stand elegantly above the floating city, the once-silent city clamored like a tsunami.

Whether they were admiring Anita's beauty, or that *something* symbolized by the hologram—and it was something close to an ideal—the acclamation from Aphrodite rose ever higher.

The hologram seemed to be telling them all—silently—that while the floating city Aphrodite was full of contradictions, it was still a place to be proud of.

Anita's hologram image, surrounded by upside-down holographic waves, stood above Aphrodite.

An elegant, quiet, slightly mysterious smile hovered on her lips....

Yūichi looked up at Anita's hologram from his cabin in Herleg. Where he had been hit by the boys hurt a lot, and he had had to leave Gil and Voight and come home alone. But when he saw Anita's hologram, his regret at missing the Festival evaporated.

Yūichi was intoxicated. He forgot his black and blue marks, and worshiped Anita's hologram.

The friendship Gil and Voight had shown, and this festival—what a fantastic night... Yūichi was sure he had made the right choice when he decided to live in Aphrodite permanently.

Yūichi was happy. Absurdly, incredibly happy.

He was so drunk with happiness that he didn't notice the telephone ringing behind him for some time.

▲

Voight was lying face-up on the bed.

His face was hard like pottery, with no sign of blood, and looked cold. His unshaven beard looked like a shadow. His eyes were closed. He wasn't moving.

Voight was dead.

Yūichi, who had rushed to the hospital ward, stood speechless in the doorway for a long, silent moment.

Gil was sitting on the bed—the sound of him sobbing sounded strangely unreal to Yūichi's ears.

2023 :: Age 23

"What . . . ?" his voice squeezed out at last.

"I don't know," sobbed Gil, brokenly. "An EV suddenly went out of control. . . . By the time I knew what was happening, Voight had been knocked flying. . . . How could it happen? . . . How could that accident . . . Oh, shit, shit shit!"

". . ."

Yūichi looked with empty eyes at Gil's silhouette—for some reason, memories of Voight's actions today came rushing into his mind. The Voight who had asked to be given any information concerning Mr. Caan . . . The Voight who had jumped into a fight to save Yūichi . . . The Voight who had come to the Laugh Cat with Anita . . .

"Hey! Anita!" said Yūichi in an imbecilic voice. "Did you tell Anita?"

"Hell, no!" Gil's face showed his feeling. "I can't say that to Anita. No! Hell, no!"

"I'll tell her family," came a voice from behind them. "I've already told her father, and I'm having someone contact her mother now. . ."

It was Mr. Caan's voice.

Yūichi turned and nodded dumbly, without being able to understand why Mr. Caan was there, even doubting he actually was there.

Yūichi murmured a mindless assent.

He nodded slightly, and made to leave the hospital room, as if a piece of him had been ripped out of his heart. He felt he shouldn't leave, like he had forgotten to do something, a feeling he couldn't explain even to himself.

Maybe he just couldn't bear being here, with the reality of Voight's death before his eyes.

"Wait." Mr. Caan's voice stopped him.

Yūichi waited. Yūichi had no will of his own now.

He recalled dimly that Mr. Caan had been a friend of Voight's father since a long time ago.

"Maybe I shouldn't say this here, now, but, . . ." Mr. Caan murmured, then thought a minute before continuing. "I have decided to resign as Mayor of Aphrodite. I'm too old, and quite a few people want me out. . . . I'll guess I'll have to dispose of the *Rosebud*; I can't hope to be able to maintain a submersible from now on. . . . If you don't mind not being a boat boy, I wouldn't mind if you moved into my home and lived with me. Still, I think you should seriously consider finding a different job, for the future."

". . ."

Yūichi lowered his head again, and left the hospital room, leaving them behind him: Mr. Caan; Gil, sobbing; and Voight . . . dead.

He really should think seriously about what Mr. Caan had said; but at the moment, he just didn't care about anything. He couldn't think anything. He didn't want to think anything.

Yūichi stood for a minute after leaving the hospital room, unable to decide where to go.

Then he began to walk on heavy feet.

If there was anywhere he should go, it was only to the Laugh Cat.

▲

There were no customers in the Laugh Cat.

Chairs were scattered at random across the trash-scattered floor, looking incomplete: as if they had chased out the customers and closed in a rush.

Clearly, Tarloff had been told about Voight's death, and was gone, to the hospital.

2023 :: Age 23

Still, Sue was there.

Sue, cleaning up the tables, stiffened when Yūichi came into the restaurant. Yūichi and Sue stood for a while, saying nothing; they just looked each other in the face.

"I . . . I . . ." At last, Sue tried to say something, but the words stuck in her mouth. "Voight . . ."

Yūichi understood totally what Sue was trying to say. She was grieving over Voight's death, and empathized with Yūichi, who had lost a close friend—the tears floating in Sue's eyes spoke the truth more eloquently than any words.

And then, the tension inside Yūichi snapped. Yūichi cried. He bawled like a child.

He bawled like a child, with his head buried in Sue's breast, held tight; but he knew he wasn't only crying about Voight's death.

The sadness of a season passing; the end of his adolescence . . . The pummeling force of a rootless but certain foreboding that the future—that everything—would be bad from now on: that was why he was crying.

2028 :: Age 28

▲▲▲▲   1

YŪICHI OPENED HIS EYES.

He didn't feel like getting up just yet.

He vaguely thought of all that had happened since he had come to Aphrodite.

He smiled; deep, slightly sad wrinkles appeared around his mouth.

He noticed that he was almost addicted to reminiscing, these days. They weren't memories that praised him much. Considering he was twenty-eight years old, he wasn't too healthy, and a bit too eager to avoid being involved.

Well, there was no help for it.

It was like alcohol and cigarettes. You knew it wasn't healthy, but you had to do it anyway.

Now?

Thinking about now wouldn't bring him anything, he thought, and didn't have much value in itself.

Finally, he sat up.

When he did, his arm touched Sue's naked back. Sue, mumbling something deep in her mouth, curled up and wormed back into the blankets like an oyster.

Yūichi, a bit surprised, looked down at Sue. Even though almost five years had passed since Sue had started staying over in Yūichi's room once or twice a week, he still couldn't get used to it. He always felt a slight confusion that the woman sleeping in bed with him should be Sue, and not Anita.

A foolish illusion.

First of all, Anita had been Voight's wife, and after he had died, she hadn't entered into any "special" relationship with Yūichi, not even once.

If Anita knew Yūichi was thinking that, she'd certainly laugh. Maybe she'd get angry.

Still, Yūichi yet felt it was a kind of injustice that the woman sleeping with him shouldn't be Anita.

Which wasn't to say he didn't love Sue. Quite the opposite—when he looked at Sue sleeping at his side, he choked up with the pain of how much he needed this woman. Yūichi truly loved Sue.

But he couldn't understand her.

He didn't know what she thought, or why she was continuing this relationship with him. He felt sure she loved him, but that love had a kind of coldness, like formality to a stranger. It had been that way from the first.

He wasn't dissatisfied with it, and he didn't intend to accuse her of indifference. In the real world, not everyone could be the heroes and heroines of a melodrama.

He felt the fragility of their relationship: it wouldn't be strange for it to end at any time. And perhaps because of that fragility, this slightly unusual relationship had seen Sue staying overnight in his room for five years, without them living together. Their relationship was open and free, and had none of the troubles so common to couples. He couldn't deny, though, that he felt a formless sadness.

He tried to be careful, but when he got out of bed, he woke her up after all.

2028 :: Age 28

Her breathing changed.

Yūichi waited quietly next to the bed in the thin predawn light.

"You're up already?" Sue finally spoke, with her back still to Yūichi. "You're going?"

That was a tiny private rule between them. When Yūichi got up to go to work, Sue—left alone in bed—always asked if he was leaving. It was a question rich in feeling, but still hurt: *you're leaving me already....*

"Mm," Yūichi nodded. "It's a nothing job, but if I don't do it—or something—I won't be able to eat."

"You shouldn't talk about your own work that way."

"Hey, it's the truth."

"It's work that somebody has to do."

"It's work that anybody could do."

"I wash dishes every day at the Laugh Cat," said Sue, with her back turned, as always, to Yūichi. Her voice sounded a bit moist, a bit muffled. "Maybe anybody could do it, but I don't think I'm doing a nothing job."

"..."

"Right?"

"Sleep well, Sue," said Yūichi gently. "Just leave the key in the usual place."

"You're going?"

"Mm."

Yūichi stretched out his hand, and stroked Sue's hair tenderly. For some reason, he felt his love rise into a lump in his throat.

Sue twisted her neck, and looked Yūichi full in the face.

She lay breathing quietly in the bed, looking up at Yūichi, taking the quiet and the dimness to her and transforming into a strange and rare animal.

Yūichi laughed brightly, and waved lightly to Sue. Then he left the bedroom.

▲

True, it was work that had to be done by someone, but it wasn't true it could be done by just anyone.

It was work that required a great deal of endurance, the endurance to withstand the humiliation of playing nursemaid to a robot.

The sea around Aphrodite required constant dredging.

No cause had been put forward yet—maybe it was because of the heat radiating from Aphrodite, maybe because its giant structure was disrupting the ocean currents—but in any case, the giant whirlpool under the city had been increasing in frequency with the years, and its destructive power was immense.

As a result, the rate of mud deposition on the ocean bed had increased, and without dredging it would soon reach the point where it would impact Aphrodite's function.

Deep-sea mobile robots, or 'mobots', had a diameter of 1.5 meters, a height of 4.5 meters, a submerged weight of 1.8 tons, and were equipped with both sonar and a television camera for senses, and a gyroscope for attitude control. Of course, they also had manipulators for undersea work.

The mobot, connected by cable to the mother ship, worked under remote control. This mobot, teamed up with a seabed bulldozer and an OSPER (OceanoSPace explorER), undertook the dredging work. On this team, the humans didn't play all that

2028 :: Age 28

important a role. Really, they had no role at all. . . . Even the commands from the ship were made by a computer based on the OSPER's pattern recognition feedback.

So what was Yūichi doing there?

On the dredging barge—less than three hundred tons—he scraped off the mud that had accumulated on the aluminum alloy surfaces of the robots.

He laboriously cleaned the mud off with an aluminum scraper and a hose, after the mobot had been lifted onto the deck by a giant crane.

It was extremely monotonous, but not at all easy; and it was a job where, more than anything, you had to withstand the humiliation of having your position and that of the robot reversed.

Anybody would look down on it as a nothing job, not just Yūichi. Still, Yūichi was happy to have found even that work.

Aphrodite was trapped in a severe depression, and the number of jobless on the streets was increasing. Including all the people out of work but not actively searching any more, the total unemployment rate was probably over thirty percent. And there were a lot of people who wanted to work, but couldn't.

The direct cause was supposed to be that there were now so many ocean factories. Aphrodite had lost its value as the only ocean resource development factory. The city finances were tight, and Mr. Caan's ideals for the construction of Aphrodite—which had never been clearly communicated to the city residents—had ended in total failure.

It was like a stone tumbling down a slope.

After Mr. Caan resigned as mayor, the character of Aphrodite as a semi-independent state rapidly began to unravel, left unprotected. Finally, Aphrodite became so weak that it couldn't exist without outside aid.

Herself sector was filled with hotels built with foreign capital; and even much of the land in Herleg had been sold to foreign realtors by the city government. Recently, there was a rumor that Aphrodite was going to be used as a military base by one of the major powers.

... Just like a stone tumbling downhill.

Yūichi couldn't forget the glory of Aphrodite and those sparkling, sun-filled days, couldn't believe what had happened—how could such a thing ever happen? He still believed that the depression, and even the government that was nothing more than a yes-man for a major power, were just temporary aberrations, and that the vibrant energy of Aphrodite would be reborn.

Of course, that wasn't true. It wasn't even *optimistic*—it just totally ignored the reality of the situation.

The fact was that Aphrodite was decaying, just floating into desolation.

But Yūichi couldn't accept that. To accept that would be to admit that his youth was lost forever. He couldn't bear that.

While working on the dredge, he saw a bulldozer tear down a section of Herleg sector, and couldn't entirely suppress a feeling, an omen, of uneasiness. He felt afraid, wondering what would become of Aphrodite.

Yūichi didn't realize it, but that fear was rooted deep inside himself, and that was why he was scared to look at reality, instead fleeing into nostalgia.

If nothing else happened, Yūichi would become a

2028 :: Age 28

passive, dull worshiper of the past, and that would be all.

If nothing else happened....

The mobot was hoisted up by the crane.

For an instant, the water poured from its aluminum body like a waterfall. The mobot swayed a little, then stopped, suspended in space.

The cable ran out, and the mobot slowly settled down onto the deck. It wouldn't be good if the 3.2 ton robot fell and punched a hole though the deck!

The barge tilted a bit as the mobot settled, and the water spray started.

The high-pressure jet sprayed over the mobot, sluicing the mud away before his eyes. The mobot recalled the stern figure of a king—its manipulators crossed over its chest, immobilized in the crossing streams of water.

As abruptly as they had started, the streams of water stopped, leaving the deck wet as after a sudden monsoon.

Yūichi and the other man lifted their aluminum scrapers and started on the mobot. They removed the seaweed twisted around the manipulators and began to scrape off the mud.

The screeching of the aluminum alloy scraper set his teeth on edge, but there wasn't much point in complaining. It was work.

In the sizzling sunshine, steam rose from the puddles on the deck. They were drenched in sweat within seconds in that humid heat, dripping from the ends of their noses, from their elbows.

Yūichi kept doggedly to his work, apparently not even noticing the heat. His youth was still evident in the rhythmical movements of his muscles.

After Yūichi finished scraping the mud from the mobot's base, he climbed to the top of the stepladder, and began to scrape the head—Yūichi liked moving his body, so the work wasn't such a burden. Without even that much, the perverted sight of a human working for a robot would surely be unbearable.

Compared to Yūichi, the other worker had no will to work at all. He was idly moving his scraper, as if in apology, but of course no mud fell off under that weak pressure. It was a desultory, almost sullen working style.

A middle-aged, somehow vulgar man—this was the first time Yūichi had been teamed with him.

"Damn job don't pay enough...." He discarded his scraper onto the deck, and spit out the words. "Stingy."

Yūichi looked down at the man from the mobot's shoulder, and he began to get a little angry. Then his expression softened, as if he changed his mind, and he asked, "What's up?"

"I said the job don't pay enough," the man snapped. "And you feel the same, right?"

"Hey, even if I do, there's not much you can do about it..."

"You give in pretty easy for a young punk." He lifted up a hand to point at the purple silhouette of Aphrodite spreading out beyond the wave dampers.

"I can't give up. I was hooked by an immigration poster, and there's nothing to do. A tight-fisted nothing island... I was tricked. And you want me to give in?"

Yūichi was silent.

The old Yūichi would have leaped to attack any-

2028 :: Age 28

one who bad-mouthed Aphrodite. That fire had burned out, though, and he couldn't argue with the fact that Aphrodite was a tight-fisted little isle.

Too bad, but it was true.

"It had its good times." Yūichi had to say at least that much in defense of Aphrodite. "Aphrodite had really good times...."

"Me, I came here about five years ago." The man looked the other way, with contempt on his face, and spat towards Aphrodite. "It was for the Twentieth Anniversary Festival. I came about two days before. Since then Aphrodite has just got worse and worse. Thanks to that, look at me now.... I can't believe that Aphrodite ever had good times."

He stopped for a minute, then spoke as if affirming it to himself, "I just can't believe it."

His voice held the special hatred of a man swallowed by bad luck. He was probably the kind of person who would be dogged by bad luck wherever he was. He was born a whipped dog.

In any case, though, his words had certainly hit the mark.

The Festival five years ago—the glory of Aphrodite had been at peak tide then. Even then the city had embraced many contradictions, but no one thought they would be mortal wounds, and they had all thought, optimistically, that they would be resolved.

Aphrodite had reached the peak of its glory at the Festival, and, as if that had been a borderline, began to follow the path to decay. Voight had died, Mr. Caan had resigned as mayor—everything began to turn for the worse.

Yūichi didn't want to show his welling tears, so he turned his face away from the other man, and returned to his scraping work.

"What the! . . . Right in the middle of a damn conversation, . . ." he muttered. As if spurred by the words, he bent to pick up the scraper he had dropped to the deck.

Just then, it happened.

Suddenly he was thrown into the air, feet leaving the ladder. Yūichi fell flailing through space, flipped, and crashed onto his back on the deck. He rolled along as he hit.

The dredge pointed its prow to the sky, surged upward again, and then collapsed the other way like a roller coaster. Sheets of water, split by the profile of the huge stern crane, came falling to the deck with a roar.

His hand shot out in reflex, and barely caught the handrail—he would have been washed into the sea.

Yūichi stood up, slipped and fell, and stood again.

Like a bath after the plug had been pulled, the sea drew into a funnel-shaped whirlpool, tattered in foam, and bared its triangular teeth. The giant waves that smashed into the ship made it resonate like a drum.

The dredge repeated its up-down piston movement, and was buried under the waves several times. Spray hung like fog, and his field of vision was nil.

Yūichi hung onto the handrail for dear life. Every time the waves came crashing down on his head, he lost his balance again, and knew he would be thrown overboard if he loosened his grip.

Memories of the submersible competition with Gil came flashing back. The same whirlpool that had savaged their submersibles then was now battering the dredge, but on a scale many times worse.

2028 :: Age 28

There was something awesome in the whirlpool's energy. It had the destructive power of a giant bomb—but while Yūichi was terrified of it, he felt a strange kind of exhilaration. Every time he was battered by the waves, his memories of that submersible race returned even more vividly.

Each time the dredge was pulled towards the sea-bottom prow first, each time the waves came rushing in, he laughed! He was possessed by the illusion that the dredge was Mr. Caan's submersible, the *Rosebud*.

From between the high-leaping waves, bending in like fangs, the sun-filled, clear blue sky of the South Pacific came peeping in.

Suddenly he heard the sound of a cable zipping over metal, overlaid by a shrieking voice. He turned, and saw the sinking mobot and the figure of the other man, desperately struggling in the sea.

It was obvious what had happened.

First the mobot, and then the man—whose legs had been caught in the cables—had fallen into the sea. With cables were wrapped around his legs he couldn't move freely, and he would surely drown together with the mobot.

There was no time to dither.

Keeping his hands on the rail, he worked his way back to the pilothouse, step by step.

Luckily, the whirlpool was already dissipating, and except for the wet slippery deck, it was no great trouble to walk.

The man peering out of the pilothouse saw Yūichi, and shouted in surprise, "What the hell are you doing walking around? You're gonna get washed off!"

Yūichi ignored him, and flung himself off the

handrail into the pilothouse, shoving the man away with his elbow.

"Hey, you can't touch that!" the other shouted, but by then Yūichi had already punched the control button.

He glanced over his shoulder to check that the cables had separated from the crane, and the mobot was sinking into the sea—the man, on the verge of drowning, was free of the cables, but didn't seem to have the strength left to swim himself.

Yūichi jumped from the pilothouse, leapt the handrail—and dove into the sea.

2

Yūichi rubbed the rough towel against his chest with all his might.

It made a sound like polishing leather shoes, evidence his muscles were still firm enough. They didn't make him feel twenty-eight years old, and that made him so happy that he kept rubbing his bare chest even after his skin was red and began to sting.

Yūichi was grinning.

More than rescuing a man from drowning, the fact that he had leapt into the sea without hesitating made him happier, and much prouder.

When he dove into the sea, he had proven to himself that he was still young, that he still had the power to succeed at what he wanted to do.

To the Yūichi who was surrounded by a decaying Aphrodite; to the Yūichi who felt that his life had ended, that was a fresh joy, a discovery.

Somehow, that vivid rescue was a chance for life to return again to the battered Yūichi who had been lost in nostalgia.

The sound of rubbing leather.

Yūichi was rubbing his bare chest with the towel. As if a new Yūichi would be born through it, he continued to rub.

The door behind Yūichi opened, and the work boss' face peered in.

An amazing thing. For the work boss to show his face here, in this room reserved for the mud-scrapers, was rare indeed.

"Will you come to the sick bay?" asked the work boss. "Seegar is asking for you, wants to thank you. It looks like he has something to ask you, too...."

Seegar was the name of the man Yūichi had rescued.

"Yes, sir," Yūichi nodded, threw the towel over the chair, and began to put on his shirt quickly. As he was buttoning his shirt, he noticed the work boss was still standing behind him, and stopped his fingers.

"Is there something else?"

"Uh... Eh..." The work boss looked away, seemed to be at a loss as to how to say something, then spilled the words out. "They want you to quit."

Yūichi stared at the work boss. His fingers unconsciously began to button his shirt again.

"I feel for you, but..." Maybe he had relaxed after blurting it all out, but this time the work boss looked straight at Yūichi. "It's orders from above. You have to quit."

"Oh."

"Yeah."

"I'd like to know why." Yūichi spoke in a voice so level it surprised even him. "I don't remember doing anything to be fired for."

"You cut the cables and sank the mobot to the bottom. It'll cost a bundle to recover it.... That's what they said...."

"It would have been impossible to rescue Seegar without it."

"Upstairs doesn't think like that. They say there must have been another way."

2028 :: Age 28

"If there was one, I'd like to hear it. . . ." Yūichi's voice was a little ragged. "And even if there was, it wasn't likely anyone could think of it at the time."

"That's true. That's true, but . . ."

"What do you mean, 'That's true, but'? You mean the mobot is more valuable than the life of a mere mud-scraping worker?"

". . ." The work boss fell silent again, and looked the other way. He was embarrassed, and looked very alone.

There was a dangerous silence between them for a while.

"Yes, sir. I understand," said Yūichi finally. "I'll resign."

"It's orders from above, I can't do anything. It's orders from above. . . ." The work boss mumbled those words deep in his mouth, but made no effort to lift his head. Maybe he was afraid of meeting Yūichi's eyes.

Yūichi turned on his heel, straightened his back, and left the room. The wonderful feeling of a few minutes before had vanished from Yūichi's heart. Still, it wasn't as if the bad luck of losing his job would batter him down. It was nothing more than coldly recognizing the fact that the time had come to set his foot on the path to a new life.

He didn't have any idea yet what kind of life it might be. . . .

▲

Not too many people could say precisely what part of Herhip had changed, or how. The people living in Herhip felt the changes vaguely, but had little interest in them, and to the people on the outside, it was just another narrow, jumbled-up district.

But the omens of change were clearly visible here, and the changes were even greater than those occurring in Herself, or Herleg.

The thing that made Herhip into *Herhip*—the raw power of life, raw hunger, whatever you called it—was slowly but unquestionably leaching away.

Herhip sector was valuable exactly because it was a boiling pot of different ethnic groups, good and bad, all mixed together, and its wicked vitality too, had meaning.

After Herhip lost its anarchic vitality, all that was left was a slum.

The first to notice were the Chinese immigrants, then the Indian merchants, and they began to withdraw from Herhip sector. They cut themselves away from Herhip, fleeing as if from a shipwrecked vessel.

On the surface very little of this change was visible. As before, there was pickpocketing and theft, prostitutes grabbed people brazenly, and there was laughter on the streets—but like a spreading mold, the sunken belt of lost vitality was spreading.

Yūichi understood it well.

Today, walking through Herhip sector brought no sense of bubbling exuberance: you couldn't feel it any more. It seemed almost as if putrescence were drifting in the air.

Yūichi was walking through Herhip to visit Seegar's home, to pick up some necessities like underwear and things.

Seegar had smashed his chest against the ship's side, and was going to be in the hospital for a while. Since he had nobody close to him, Yūichi felt he had no choice but to bring him all the things he needed in the hospital.

2028 :: Age 28

Yūichi walked along the harbor cobblestones.

The moored fishing boats of all sizes, the odor of fish in his nose; these were the same as before, but he somehow couldn't feel any vitality here. It was as if the essence had been squeezed out, leaving nothing but the lusterless dregs.

In the clear sunlight and the bright sea, the more Herhip glittered in the sun, the more it looked vacant, unbalanced.

The cobblestone road swung away from the harbor, and became a rising slope.

Houses of different styles lined both sides of the slope road, overhanging like eyelids, making a strange and jumbled skyline.

Maybe it was his imagination, but there seemed to be fewer children than before.

At the top of the hill was a small open space with a huge eucalyptus. There were two benches, and a single small brick flowerbed—surprisingly unprepossessing for Herhip sector.

A small crowd loitered there, staring fixedly at the sea. Expressionless, they seemed transient as shadows; barely aware of their own existence.

Yūichi slowly looked back over his shoulder, and saw what they were looking at.

In the shining blue sea, a single black speck, a nuclear submarine, had appeared, and was slowly approaching Aphrodite.

It was an 8,000-ton displacement class submarine, equipped with two 20-centimeter heat blasters, six 50-centimeter atomic torpedo ports, and eighteen MRBM missiles.

From this distance, it was impossible to tell what flag it was flying. No doubt it was either American or NATO.

Aphrodite

That Aphrodite was being used as a naval fleet base by various countries hadn't been officially announced, but people were already starting to accept the fact that nuclear carriers and submarines were making port calls.

Yūichi couldn't take his eyes off the nuclear submarine either.

The submarine was black, and evil. Its oppressive shape seemed to foretell the end of the time when Aphrodite could protect its status as a semi-independent state. It signaled that the time had come when Aphrodite could only continue to exist as a mere pawn in the game of politics. . . .

This nuclear submarine bluntly signaled that the Aphrodite of the past and the Aphrodite of the here and now were different: the Aphrodite he loved was no more. No doubt the other people watching the submarine were feeling the same thing. They reminded him suddenly of a funeral procession, with that empty-hearted sense of loss floating on their expressionless faces.

Yūichi suddenly felt he couldn't bear to be there any longer. He turned and left the area quickly.

Seegar's room was near the plaza.

Seegar's room was in an especially jumbled area, even for Herhip sector, and home to a community Yūichi couldn't quite place. In one corner of the intricate, maze-like back streets was an old apartment house with one wall about to collapse. Seegar had said that was where he was living. The apartment house was dark, humid, and a sour smell floated in the air.

The decay of Aphrodite was painted thick and dark here.

2028 :: Age 28

Of course, even in the prime of Aphrodite, there had been prostitutes and ruffians, and deserted apartments like this. Still, in Herhip—and even in this out-of-the-way corner—the sun's radiance had been glorious, and people used to live in a daredevil way. It was now a miserable place, everything rotten from the core.

Seegar's room was on the third floor.

The instant Yūichi entered the room, he felt terribly depressed. That room where the sun never shone stank of rotten eggs. It told of Seegar's desolate psychology: a cold, wild room.

Yūichi knelt on the floor, and pulled the old suitcase out from under the bed. According to Seegar, everything he needed was in that suitcase.

The fasteners must have been weak, because when he lifted it the top sprang open, and the clothing spilled out onto the floor in disorder. Yūichi started to pick everything up—and stopped abruptly.

Along with the clothing, a handful of newspaper clippings and two photographs had fallen out.

Yūichi slowly pushed them together, staring at them. Possessed by a terrible suspicion, his face grew troubled.

The newspaper clippings, all of them, reported the accident that had happened to Voight five years ago, during the Twentieth Anniversary Festival. One of the photos was a snapshot of Voight, caught unawares; while the other was a photo of the man Yūichi had driven from the airport to Mr. Caan's home that morning, the man Voight had said was from the DSAA.

Yūichi remembered that Seegar had said he had come to Aphrodite a few days before the Festival.

I wonder if that really was an accident.... That

foreboding clutched his heart, and Yūichi froze at the horror of the suspicion.

From somewhere, he heard a baby crying, and the scolding, hysterical voice of its mother.

Yūichi continued to squat there, motionless, holding the pictures and the clippings in his hands.

▲▲▲▲ 3

The giant spiral building loomed up in the strong afternoon sun.

It seemed to be made of elements from spiral staircases; and when seen from a distance, it was strangely distorted, in a way that made the watcher feel vaguely uneasy.

Maybe if the building had been placed in Herself sector, it wouldn't have looked so strange and jarring. In Herself, avant-garde buildings swarmed together, achieving a strange harmony as a whole.

But here, in Herleg sector, it stood out clearly as being "different." In Herleg, a terraced town cut through the gentle hills, the perspective was always based on parallel lines, and the scenery brought an unvoiced sense of security to the viewer's heart—but that spiral building rose up thirty meters, pinched in the middle, and stretched out to the left and right for the top floors. In Herleg sector's world of parallel lines, it was an entirely foreign building; it destroyed the view. It had been built by the man they called the Hotel King of America. Not only had he bought the land for the hotel, but he had also bought massive areas of Herleg ocean front. Of course, that land was likely to end up privately-owned, open only to the hotel guests. Hotel construction was at the point of interior decoration and furnishings right now, but when it opened, countless tourists would press in from all over the world. It was no mistake that the South Seas would shine wonderfully into all their windows.

No mistake, but... it was also no mistake that the wonder of Aphrodite, as conceived by Mr. Caan when he built it, would become transformed into something vastly different.

When those hotel guests looked down on Aphrodite from the spiral hotel and said it was wonderful, their words would unquestionably hold a sense of superiority.

That a giant hotel should be built in Herleg with foreign capital—that in itself was a major offense against the very concepts of Aphrodite's construction, but no one even tried to protest it. The change in Aphrodite wasn't limited to Herleg sector, and the massive amounts of money the hotel would bring were needed by weak Aphrodite.

Yūichi was another who thought there was no help for it, that it was just something you had to accept.

Still, he was unhappy that his friend Gil was on the hotel staff. He knew it was childish, but he felt betrayed.

Gil had been a salesman at a travel agency, but his performance there had been recognized: he had been tapped by the Hotel King as a sub-manager.

Nobody, including Yūichi, had expected it, but it seemed that Gil was the successful type. When Yūichi visited Gil, he was in the middle of working, looking very busy.

Hang on a second, he signaled with one hand, earnestly typing something into the computer.

Yūichi retreated to the wall, and waited for Gil to finish.

2028 :: Age 28

It was the early afternoon, when the sunlight was strongest.

Through the window behind Gil, he could see the sun shining brilliantly, and the luxurious undulations of the dark blue sea.

Gil was devoted to his work. When you saw how he worked, you could understand why he had been given a room in the hotel as an office. There was no mistake: Gil was trusted greatly by the Hotel King.

Leaning against the wall, Yūichi lazily thought about when he and Gil had contested the right to date Anita, and that ten years had passed since they raced their submersibles.

So many things had happened in those ten years, but they had passed too quickly.

"Ah, finished." Gil tapped out a firm, final keystroke, then stood up. Then he saw the suitcase Yūichi was holding, and his eyes bulged.

"What!? You? Are you planning to travel somewhere?"

"Nope. The suitcase isn't mine," said Yūichi, shaking his head. "Is it OK? You look pretty busy."

"Well, busy... I'm always busy. Don't worry about it," said Gil, punching his own shoulder to relax stressed muscles. "Same with you, huh?"

"Nope."

"You should be busy," nodded Gil to himself. "You have to be busy. The two of us aren't boat boys any more."

"I got fired."

Gil stopped his fist in mid-air, and looked at Yūichi. "Really?" he asked. "Oh."

Gil's eyes looked like he was lost in thought for a minute, then he finally sighed and said "If you came to ask for a job, I'm sorry, but..."

"Not for that."

"You'd hate this job. You don't like it that Aphrodite is changing. However much we're friends, you can't expect me to press my boss for . . ."

"Listen to me."

Gil fell silent, pressured.

"I don't want a job," said Yūichi, quietly, as if pushing his point home. "I came for a different reason."

"Different?"

"Uh huh."

"That's good." Gil gave a bitter smile. "That's real good."

"That's good." Yūichi hadn't intended it, but there was cynicism in his voice.

"That's real good," repeated Gil, in a challenging voice, lifting his face. "Yeah, it's good . . . I don't know if you believe me, but I loved Aphrodite too. I was lost in it. . . . But Aphrodite's changed. No helping it. We've got no choice but to change with it. It would be a lot easier to live hanging on to the old Aphrodite, but I don't want that lifestyle . . . I don't like your type of person, who lives only looking at the past. It's meaningless. Because you live like that, you . . ."

" . . .I'm even a failure at cleaning mud from a mobot, right?" said Yūichi softly, picking up Gil's words.

Gil fell silent for an instant, with nothing to say, then firmed his jaw. "You are my friend. But that doesn't mean I accept your lifestyle . . . and I can't recommend anyone to the company whose lifestyle I don't accept."

"I know," nodded Yūichi. "I understand all that."

They both fell silent for a minute, then Gil spoke as if to hide the uneasiness of that silence.

2028 :: Age 28

"You said you had something to talk about. What?"

"About Voight."

"Voight?"

"Yeah. There's something that's bothering me a little," Yūichi nodded, and asked, "When Voight had his accident, he was in the middle of going to meet someone, right?"

"Aah... He said he had to go meet someone who was going to supply him with some information. I didn't ask who, or what kind, because it wasn't my business.... He was totally engrossed in his work."

"And in the middle of going to meet this person who was going to give him information, he was struck and killed by a runaway driverless car...."

"Mm... The police said they couldn't understand why the car suddenly started up, either."

Gil's face grew troubled. "A terrible accident... But it's not so tough to explain... Voight was my friend, too.... I still think that if Voight was going to die like that, it would have been better never to have known him at all."

For an instant, thinking of their dead mutual friend, the close friendship between Gil and Yūichi flowered again, even though they were so different in position and thinking.

"Why rehash that old story now?" asked Gil finally. "It's at least five years old."

"I said, there's something bothering me. I'll explain the details when we're together with Anita.... Did you contact her?"

"Yeah, she was just in. Lucky. She said she had something to talk about, too."

"What time is the date?"

"If we leave here now, it'll be just about right. We decided to meet in Herself...."

"Thanks." After Yūichi thanked him, he hesitated a moment, and then the words rushed out. "About what you said before, it's different, isn't it?"

"What are you talking about?" Gil brought his eyebrows together.

"You asked what I was rehashing about Voight's accident," said Yūichi, "But rehashing... As far as we go, nothing concerning Voight has ended, has it?"

"...That's right," affirmed Gil to himself after a pause. "Aphrodite's changed, you and I have both gotten five years older... Only he, only Voight, stays the same."

▲

The change in Herself sector was not as blatant as, say, that of Herhip or Herleg.

One reason was that the vertical shafts, plazas, structural and equipment floors, and giant towers of Herself were still built up like a model, and there was no space for change. Another was that the Control Tower, Information Tower, and other central facilities couldn't be removed as long as Aphrodite stood.

Only Herself still preserved the old view.

That metallic, functional beauty never faded: the monorail and the hover-buses still moved throngs of people, and everything was still as active as ever.

Still, as an apple rots from the core out, so Herself was changing from the inside, yet invisible to the eye.

The inside—the spirit of it all.

2028 :: Age 28

When Mr. Caan built Aphrodite he had respected the flexibility of the spirit, and had wanted to create a society that valued play as highly as work. Herself liberated people from the labor of making their daily bread—it was designed to provide them with an outlet from their busy, tiring daily work, and in that sense it was yet another functional part of the whole.

But that function of Herself—that it should be used by people—was gradually changed and ultimately reversed.

Maybe it was centralization of power, maybe it was the way they managed people, but in any case Herself no longer existed for the people. Quite the opposite: the people now had to work to maintain the central facilities there.

Today, Herself was unmistakably the symbol of "Authority."

Although it was still beautiful, still giant—no: perhaps precisely because it was—it dominated the people, suffocated them.

Unless Yūichi really had pressing business there, he no longer went to Herself.

That's right—unless he had, for example, an appointment with Anita, he didn't want to take even one step into Herself.

Anita had chosen a hotel lounge in Herself to meet.

The three glass walls were always opened at this hour, so you could see the sparkling sea and enjoy the fragrance of the tide while enjoying your drink. The wicker basket on the table was heaped with pineapples, papayas, bananas and the like, and the heavy, sweet smell drifted through the room—the lounge was designed to look like a lodge on a Pacific atoll.

Near the open glass wall, a large birdcage was suspended from the ceiling, housing parrots that looked like they had been splashed with oil paints. The parrots burst out every so often in strange voices that nobody could understand, and fluttered their wings. When they did, they caught the sunlight, and sent shadows rushing through the lounge that made the eyes reel, fading its colors until it looked like a scene from an old movie.

You could hear the polite whispering of many people. Purple smoke floated. The faint clink of coffee cups on saucers . . .

The lounge had a special, relaxing quality, an atmosphere that made you feel good. Within that goodness, though, there was something almost irritating. There was something, somewhere, that didn't fit Aphrodite—Yūichi didn't like it.

Anita finally came, ten minutes late.

Anita, too, had changed. Not to say that she wasn't beautiful. Quite the opposite. With every passing day, Anita grew more beautiful, more enchanting, more refined.

Compared to the first time Yūichi had met her, she was like a stranger. Even the Anita who had been selected as Aphrodite "Aphrodite" had still been childish in comparison—Anita was supernatural, proud, and so, so youthful. While he felt no foolish dreams about her, he hadn't lost all hope, either: hadn't let reality become meaningless. They almost never mentioned dead Voight.

Anita came walking over to their table with animated but refined footsteps. The desirous glances of all the men in the lounge focused on her; but she

2028 :: Age 28

walked directly across the floor, her head high, her heels clicking, as if she were walking on a deserted plain.

After she kissed Yūichi and Gil on the cheeks, she sat down slowly. She rested her chin on the backs of her hands, tilted her head a little, and looked at the two of them.

"I haven't seen you for a long time," she said. "It must be over a year now."

"Two years," said Gil, baring his teeth like a horse taking an offered piece of grass. "What with one thing and another, two years..."

"Have you been well?"

"Mm... How about you?"

"I've been very well. I've moved twice, taken French lessons, and bankrupted a newspaper."

"Don't you have any help to rebuild the *Aphrodite Facsimile*?"

"I don't have Voight's talent." Anita shrugged lightly. "Voight's father has passed away, too, and even if there were a purpose to restarting it, I don't feel like doing it."

She shifted her vision to Yūichi, and changed her tone of voice a little.

"Are the Laugh Cat's Tarloff and Sue well?"

"Yeah,..." nodded Yūichi, sipping his coffee to disguise the bad taste in his mouth. "They're doing fine. Tarloff's gone white at the temples."

The conversation flagged for a minute.

Anita had ordered grapefruit juice from the waiter, and was playing with the straw that had come with it, in her long smooth fingers. Her nails had been neatly manicured and painted.

"So, what do you have to talk about?" she asked finally.

"Um." Yūichi stroked his chin, and hesitated a minute. "It'd be better to finish your story first. Mine is a little complicated."

"Oh." Anita shifted her eyes to the entrance, rose up a little, and lifted a hand. "Over here!"

Yūichi and Gil turned, and saw a muscular young man walking towards them. He was wearing a spotless suit, and smiling as if he was so happy he couldn't bear it.

Yūichi and Gil, surprised, rose slightly in their seats to greet him. "Nice place!" said the man in a big voice, standing at the side of the table. "Nice feel to it!"

Then he bent over and kissed Anita's cheek. Anita smiled.

"This is David," said Anita. "This is Yūichi, and Gil . . . My very good friends."

"Glad to meet you," he said in his big voice, holding out his right hand.

"Hi," said Yūichi, as Gil mumbled "The pleasure's mine." Neither of them felt at ease, as they shook his hand. They had absolutely no idea why they were greeting this man.

"David is a specialist in economics," said Anita.

"My specialty is computers," corrected David. "I'm just working for a New York economic research institute."

"Did you come to Aphrodite on vacation?" asked Yūichi.

He had to ask something, even that, to keep the conversation moving.

"No, on work." David shook his head. "I was sent by the economic research institute to examine Aphrodite's economic condition, and to write a report on the appropriate solution.

2028 :: Age 28

"We've been engaged by the Aphrodite government."

"Oh, really?" nodded Yūichi, noncommittally.

"Yes," smiled David. "I've spent three months here, and I'm returning to New York next week."

"And how is the economic condition of Aphrodite?" asked Gil. "Do you think we can ever beat down the inflation?"

"Probably useless." David shook his head. "Even if you do manage to break the inflation, under the present conditions, it will just exhaust Aphrodite's finances. Aphrodite is caught between being a tourist spot and a floating factory complex. If Aphrodite doesn't choose one of the two roles, its continued existence as a city is going to be very difficult."

"What do you think is the most effective?"

"Resources, capital, and labor must all be placed under absolute management. You must advocate and push planned production and planned consumption."

"But that's . . ." Yūichi started to speak without planning to. "That's totalitarianism, isn't it?"

David ran his eyes over Yūichi, smiled, and spoke as an expert. "For the continued existence of Aphrodite, even that is not enough. Maybe you're thinking you can survive here if Aphrodite becomes a floating factory complex, but the future for floating factories is none too bright either. Asteroid mining has reached the point where it's on a firm commercial basis, and it's cheaper than ocean mining. Most people think the opposite, but sending a rocket to the moon is easier than working in the ocean at two thousand meters. From the viewpoint of materials, too, space development uses aluminum alloy, ultra-tensile steel, plastic, and various types of titanium; but at two thousand meters you can't use those materials. The pressure per square inch is unbelievably high."

Yūichi fell silent.

If asteroid mining was cheaper than ocean mining, then no matter how you looked at it, Aphrodite had lost its reason to exist. David hadn't said it in as many words, but he seemed sure that Aphrodite was doomed.

"What about its future as a tourist spot?"

"Too bad, but not much of a future there, either," shrugged David. "It's a problem of the capacity to accept visitors. You don't want a big flow. From a personal point of view . . ."

David cut the flow of his words there a moment, turned to face Anita, and lightly squeezed her arm. "I love Aphrodite. The sea, the wind, these bewitching women . . ."

Yūichi was silent. There was no need to ask. The way he looked at Anita told the entire story.

"Excuse me for a minute," said David, standing. "I'm expecting a call from New York . . . I'll be back in about twenty minutes." He sent a well-bred smile towards Yūichi and Gil, and after touching Anita's cheek with his finger strode out of the lounge. An uncomfortable silence descended on the three people left at the table.

"I'm leaving Aphrodite," announced Anita finally, as if a decision had been made.

"You're going together?" asked Gil, somewhat hesitantly.

"Mm . . ."

"To New York?"

"To New York."

"Going to marry him?"

2028 :: Age 28

"I plan to."

"That's..." Gil bogged down, coughed a little, then continued. "That's wonderful. I wish you both the best of luck, really."

"Thank you."

Anita dropped her eyes, and stirred her juice with her straw.

The ice made a clear tinkle, and the grapefruit seeds slowly swirled around the glass.

"...Congratulations," said Yūichi; but doubted he had spoken in a level voice. He thought his brow was probably wrinkled. Heck, he figured this shock was even greater than when Voight and Anita had announced their engagement.

Yūichi drank his coffee cup dry, and stared at a point on the table. There was something that just didn't fit, that he just didn't understand.

"Maybe this is none of my business, but..." Yūichi asked in a slow voice. "Do you really want to?"

"Yes." Anita lifted her face from the glass, and looked straight at Yūichi.

"Can you really leave Aphrodite?" asked Yūichi, unconsciously averting his eyes from hers. He never could bear to look her right in the eye. It was too radiant for him.

"I thought you loved Aphrodite. Won't you regret it if you leave?"

Anita began to stir her drink again with the straw. The melted ice gave off a strange noise, and sank to the bottom of the juice. "I don't think so," she said finally, in a relaxed voice. "I won't regret it."

"You're sure you're not forcing it?" asked Yūichi, pursuing the point. "You want to forget about Voight, so..."

"Shut up!" Gil forcibly tried to cut off Yūichi's words. "Stop it. We don't have any right to say anything like that!"

"It's OK." Anita quieted both Gil and Yūichi with those words. Her voice was gentle, but there was the twang of tensed strength in it, the twang of a stranger.

"It's OK." repeated Anita, this time in a much more relaxed voice. She shifted her gaze, and watched the slowly undulating blue sea on the other side of the glass wall.

"I loved Aphrodite,..." she said. "When Voight first led me here, I thought such a wonderful island couldn't exist... But since Voight's death, my thoughts have changed, little by little. I feel differently now...."

The sun had dropped quite a bit closer to the horizon. Shafts of soft sunlight pierced in, bathing Anita's pure, youthful profile in clear orange light. Yūichi suddenly recalled the Anita he had first met, and the Anita selected Aphrodite "Aphrodite", and was possessed by an insane desire to embrace those graceful shoulders.

Of course, he couldn't. Yūichi didn't have the right. For everything, it was too late.

"I've come to think it's different," she repeated, as if whispering to herself, then continued. "I've come to think that this city is a toy for men—no, for boys... Living in a toy town is fun, wonderful. But I'm a woman. I can't go on playing with the boys in a play town... I used to love Aphrodite, but now I hate it."

Yūichi and Gil were silent.

With a sigh, the three glass walls began to close, probably because it was so late in the afternoon. It

2028 :: Age 28

made you think of a stage somehow, with the curtain closing.

Yūichi and Gil were silent.

Yūichi had the feeling, very strongly, that he had been through all this before, years ago. He couldn't quite recall exactly what it had been.

"I'm going to look for David," said Anita, smiling, standing up from the table gracefully. "Could you handle the check?"

"Gladly," said Gil, standing up with Yūichi. They both shook hands with Anita.

"You said you had something to talk about. I wonder what it was," said Anita, shaking Yūichi's hand.

"It doesn't matter," said Yūichi smiling. "It wasn't important. Don't worry about it."

"Oh," nodded Anita, and moved back from Yūichi. Then, in a voice that was so bubbly it sounded false, she said "Well . . . We might not meet again, so, the two of you, stay well."

"You too."

"I wish you every happiness."

Anita turned her back to them, and left the lounge in her stately walk.

Yūichi was suddenly aware that the smell of oleander was reborn in his nostrils.

He recalled then, that when Mrs. Caan had left Aphrodite, it had been just the same.

Yūichi now, finally, a decade later, could understand what Mrs. Caan had felt when she left Aphrodite.

◆◆◆◆ 4

Lit by a sad white light, the hospital room looked like a morgue. Except for Seegar, the double line of beds was empty of patients, emphasizing the loneliness. The speaker sounded every so often, echoing with the voice of a nurse paging a doctor, dismally.

Seegar was squatting on a corner of the bed, with his arms around his knees, hiding his face. His eyes darted out from behind his arms with the cowardice of a cornered rat.

"I'm not especially planning to do anything to you," said Yūichi in a patient voice, standing at the corner of the bed. "I just want to know why you have a picture of that DSAA man who came to Aphrodite, and a picture of Voight, and why you were so interested in Voight's death that you collected news clippings."

"Voight was our friend," Gil added from the side. "That's why we want to know the truth."

"I'm a sick man," whined Seegar. "Trying to interrogate a sick man is inhumane, isn't it?"

"How much do you want?" spat out Gil, irritated.

Seegar sneered, and stuck out his right hand. He put up three fingers, then seemed to reconsider, and spread it out. Five fingers.

Gil took out his billfold, and pressed five bills into

Seegar's hand. They disappeared into his pajamas like magic.

"I don't really have that much to say, . . ." whined Seegar in a husky voice, moistening his lips with his tongue.

"After I came to Aphrodite and was wandering around, a man called me over. I was handed a photo of Voight, and was told if I watched him, and reported his movements regularly, I would get some big money . . . And I was flat broke. I took the offer. . . . In another two, three days, he contacted me again, and handed me another picture, telling me to meet *this* man. I never knew until just now that he was DSAA. . . . I met him, and he said to call Voight on the night of the festival and tell him to come to a certain place."

"And did you?" Gil's voice had gone sharp. "Yeah," Seegar nodded.

"And didn't you think it might be connected with a crime?"

"Yeah, I thought so." Seegar's voice grew lower. "I said I didn't wanna be picked up for anything. So the guy in the picture—DSAA, huh?—he said, whatever happens, you'll be all right. He said if anything happened, Caan would protect me. . . ."

Gil automatically turned to face Yūichi.

Yūichi had turned white, and was frozen to the spot.

After they left the sickroom, Yūichi and Gil walked down the corridor side by side, silent. Gil deliberately stopped his feet, and said in a very tense voice, "You'd better drop it."

Yūichi stopped, and slowly turned to Gil. He was in the shadow of the white lights, and his expression couldn't be seen.

2028 :: Age 28

"What better I drop?" he asked finally in a thin voice.

"You'd better not look into Voight's death any further," said Gil. "For your own good, Yūichi."

"Can you *not* investigate?" asked Yūichi, smiling to keep from crying. "Wasn't it you who said it was meaningless to live in the past all the time? . . . Until I'm certain about how Voight died, I can't cut free of the past. I can never leave Aphrodite. . . ."

▲

Ten minutes later, Yūichi was driving an EV, or rather, riding in one.

The onboard electronics would tell the highway computer his car number and destination, delivering him to the proper place.

Yūichi didn't have to do a thing: just entrust his body to the vibrating EV.

The sun had already set behind the sea's horizon, and Herself sector was floating in resplendent lights, like a chandelier.

Yūichi, though, no longer had room in his heart to feel the beauty of it. Maybe Mr. Caan had been involved in Voight's death—and in the grip of that terrible suspicion, his heart was a long way from being able to enjoy the evening's beauty.

He felt his blood seething hot in his head. Storm winds roared deep in his ears—no mistake: if the car hadn't been automatic, he would certainly have caused an accident.

The EV rushed along, turning the highway lights into two orange snakes, crawling along the windshield.

Maybe he had to admit that Gil was a little

wiser—*Don't get me involved; I value my present life more....*

Gil had said that, and then left Yūichi—yeah, Gil was smarter. Still... Yūichi bit his lip... *Well, I just can't do it. Hell, no! If I don't meet Mr. Caan and find out the truth, I'll never move on at all....*

Just then, a fierce light suddenly shone into Yūichi's eyes.

Without any warning, another EV burst out of the ramp, and hit the body of Yūichi's car at high speed.

Fenders screeched in a wild, tooth-grating sound like a circular saw cutting steel. Sparks flew, and he could smell ozone.

Yūichi's car was slowly but definitely being pushed against the guard rail.

The siren sounded as if the computer was crazy, like the metallic scream of the EV.

For an instant, Yūichi couldn't understand what had happened. It was beyond his imagination for a contact accident to happen on the orderly Electronic Control Highway.

The far side of the car made contact with the guard rail. A metallic sound: collision. Yūichi fell forward, cutting his lip—and then the guard rail, rushing across the windshield diagonally, entered his field of vision. Beyond the guard rail, he could see the sea of reflected illumination undulating gently, quietly.

He and the car together were going to burst the guard rail and fly into the sea!

Yūichi moved instinctively, switching the automatic system to manual and accelerating.

His car dashed like a stone shot from a catapult. He opened a space between his car and the guard

2028 :: Age 28

rail as if twisting his body, and tried to cut free from his adversary.

For an instant, losing its support, the other car seemed about to smash into the guard rail itself, but barely managed a half-spin, and, righting itself, came in pursuit of Yūichi.

It was superb technique. No one who was used to driving on the automatic Electronic Control Highway could handle a car so skillfully. His opponent knew how to drive.

The other car came rushing up after Yūichi. Trying to shake him off or make him pass, Yūichi's fingers flew over the control board, frantically accelerating and decelerating. It was no use: the other, with unbelievable precision, stuck right on Yūichi's tail, and wouldn't separate.

Yūichi was seized by a sense of unreality, as if he were acting in the car chase scene in an old movie. It was so silly—he just couldn't imagine it being real. Reinforcing that sense of unreality, it was an "air pocket" time on the highway, and there wasn't another car in sight.

For a while—to Yūichi, a time measured in eternities—the two cars rushed along the highway, locked together. When Yūichi accelerated, so did the other car. When he slowed down, so did the other. It was a monotonous drive, but frightfully wearing on the nerves.

Just as over-fatigued springs break quickly, there was an instant when a space opened in his consciousness. He couldn't understand why he was driving an EV. He couldn't understand why he didn't trust the car, instead of driving it manually—under the tension, his nervous system's balance acted, almost making him lose his personal identity.

That instant of lax awareness invited irrecoverable disaster.

When Yūichi came back to his senses, the other driver had forced the nose of his own car into the space between the guard rail and Yūichi's car. Then, like a pre-ordained hammer blow, it slammed into Yūichi's vehicle.

Yūichi's car slid diagonally across the Electronic Control Highway, and finally stopped in the middle. Yūichi had smashed his chest against the dashboard when his car was hit from behind, and his entire body was numb. The pain was so sharp he almost couldn't breathe. Coughing, he curled up under the dashboard, listless.

Somewhere in his pain-fogged consciousness, a voice was warning earnestly that the side of his car was only open space.

If the other car hit him there, there would be no resistance at all. The controls and the body were destroyed, and he would be turned into bloody chopped meat.

He understood, but there was nothing he could do about it. He was beginning to come out of it, but his entire body was still numb with pain, and he couldn't even move one finger.

Yūichi lifted his face up, and screamed. He somehow managed to work his way up on top of the seat, and tried to flee from the EV. It was useless: he was a potato bug in motion. At that speed, he had no chance . . . A cry of lost hope leaked from Yūichi's throat. He hung his head, shut his eyes, and waited. Waited for the end . . .

How much time passed?

At last Yūichi opened his eyes, and stared at the ceiling of the EV in curiosity. The other car wouldn't

2028 :: Age 28

come. He was still alive—he grasped the window frame, and pulled himself up with extreme effort. He looked outside.

He saw the other car slowly going down the ramp. It was a sight that made him feel a strange sense of tranquility, like a player leaving the field after the game.

A strange, inexplicable expression floated on Yūichi's face.

Yūichi waited for the paralysis to drain from his body Then he made the car roll, and slowly went moved the ramp in pursuit of the other. It seemed just matter-of-fact. . . . The bottom of the rampway connected to the coast road.

Even though it was called the coast, it wasn't natural, of course. Fine sand was spread on the curved construction floor, and a slight curve was crafted into the overall shape of the artificial coastline.

The other EV was stopped on the coast. It was painted black against the sparkling background of triangular waves.

Yūichi maneuvered his car onto the coastline, too; and got out, walking slowly over to the other car.

He called out.

"Mr. Caan. Why didn't you kill me?"

A figure rose up out of the shadow of the car. It was Mr. Caan.

Mr. Caan was in his mid-sixties, but he looked the same as Yūichi remembered him, maybe even younger.

"When I was young, I often used to drive recklessly, . . ." Mr. Caan said in a calm voice. "My driving has gotten so insensitive lately."

"How did you find out I was coming to see you?" Yūichi's voice was rough.

"Even now, I've got many sympathizers. Someone told me you were trying to get information from Seegar. He was worried that it might become an unpleasant incident."

"You haven't answered my question."

"What question?"

"Why didn't you kill me, before?"

"From the first, I had no intention of killing you," smiled Mr. Caan bitterly. "I just thought I'd scare you a little, but even that became too much. I'm old."

They both fell silent.

The sound of the waves could be heard, and the wind had become quite strong.

"Is that you really wanted to ask me?" asked Mr. Caan at last. "Don't you want to ask me if I had anything to do with Voight's death?"

"No . . ." Yūichi automatically shook his head, confused by his own answer, a bit amazed, then set his jaw as if decided, and nodded firmly, "Yes."

It was difficult to think that Mr. Caan, whom he couldn't stop respecting, might be involved in Voight's death. But if he didn't make it clear now, he would regret it for the rest of his life.

"Back then, many nations were competing: building their own floating factory complexes, and the position of Aphrodite was worsening quickly," said Mr. Caan in an unconcerned voice.

"I wanted to maintain Aphrodite's semi-independent status at all costs. Without it, the meaning of Aphrodite's existence would vanish. . . . That's why I was considering a treaty with some of the leading powers—so that while they used Aphrodite as a naval supply base, we could enjoy advantageous conditions to develop the sea's resources. Without something like that, Aphrodite's sur-

2028 :: Age 28

vival would be difficult . . . and Voight unlocked that story. Negotiations on the final signing of the treaty had reached an extremely delicate stage, and having journalists making a lot of noise would have been fatal. I talked to the special ambassador from the DSAA who had come to Aphrodite, and asked if something couldn't be done. He said he would do something . . ."

Mr. Caan cut his words there, watched the sea for a while, and then started again.

"It doesn't really matter whether you believe me or not, but I never dreamed they would go that far. That they would murder Voight in cold blood . . . When I found out, I decided that I could no longer have any connection with Aphrodite. A blood-smeared Aphrodite was no longer my Aphrodite . . ."

Yūichi listened intently to Mr. Caan's words. No, maybe he was pretending to listen to the words, but actually was listening to the sound of the waves. The repeating, echoing sound of the waves . . .

"I understand, . . ." muttered Yūichi finally, turning to walk back towards his EV.

After a few steps, he turned to face Mr. Caan.

Mr. Caan was watching the sea. Sad, cynical, wrinkles were chiseled around his mouth. His expression suggested he was laughing at everything, including himself.

Yūichi turned his face away, and began to walk towards the EV again.

He didn't turn back a second time.

▲

When he got to the Laugh Cat, Sue was sitting at the counter, waiting for him. Tarloff was napping at a table in the corner, and there were no customers at all.

"I just got a call from the company," said Sue quietly. "They said they have to settle accounts, so they want you to drop by soon . . ."

She smiled and continued. "Congratulations! They said you were fired . . ."

"Yeah," smiled Yūichi bitterly, then turned serious. "I have something I want to talk to you about . . ."

"Like maybe you want to leave Aphrodite?"

"Uh . . ."

"Right?"

"Uh, uh-huh," Yūichi nodded, then smiled. "I'm surprised. How did you know?"

"It's obvious. You're in love with Aphrodite," she explained quietly. "But not this Aphrodite. What you love is the old Aphrodite." Sue's voice was as brave as ever, but there was an edge to it.

"So you can't stand this Aphrodite. I've thought for a while that you would decide to leave Aphrodite sometime."

"That's good," said Yūichi, relieved. "I couldn't decide how to . . ."

"There's no need to convince me of anything."

"But . . ."

"I'm not leaving Aphrodite."

"Sue!"

"I'm not leaving." Her level voice, that she had preserved up until then, was in danger of shattering. Sue took a deep breath, and stared at a point on the counter while biting her lip. Finally she spoke in a more level voice.

"Tarloff will never leave Aphrodite. He's too old; I can't leave him here alone. . . ."

2028 :: Age 28

"But still, Sue..." Yūichi was frozen, and could only shake his head, speechless.

For an instant Sue's face seemed to start to cry. When Yūichi approached to check, she twisted her body, hiding her face from him.

"Wait for me upstairs."

Then she added in a bright voice. "I'll bring whiskey and food up. Let's have a going-away party tonight, just the two of us."

She vanished into the kitchen, and Yūichi had no choice but to do as she had suggested.

The window upstairs was wide open.

▲

Herself sector, Herleg sector, Herhip sector: they were all sunk deep in the darkness, all wrapped in radiant lights, spreading out across his field of vision.

Yūichi stood at the window sill, looking out at the night view of Aphrodite.

Then he began to wave his hand, a little a first, then powerfully.

Goodbye...

Yūichi shouted it deep in his heart.

Goodbye, Voight. Goodbye Anita, Goodbye Gil, Goodbye Sue, Tarloff. Goodbye, Mr. Caan...

Goodbye... Aphrodite...

2063 :: Age 30

▲▲▲▲ 1

YŪICHI OPENED HIS EYES.

He reached out automatically, and groped in space to his upper right. The movement of his arm grew slower and at last, with a sigh, he slowly lowered it.

Realization.

This wasn't the interior of a starship, and he wasn't in a cold-sleep capsule....

He couldn't hear the beat of the metabolic clock counting out the seconds. The sighing of the oxygen pressurizer wasn't there either—instead, he could hear the sound of waves. Distant, near: only the repeated sound of the waves. Yūichi sat up on the bed, and stared for a while at the floor, not seeing it.

He thought once again that the cold sleep of a starship was hard on the nerves. It was the fear of oxygen-starvation causing brain death, the fear that you might not wake up again. That's why he couldn't free himself from the habit of reaching out to disconnect the electrodes from his head every time he woke up, even though he had been back on Earth for over a month now. Yūichi rubbed his hand over his face roughly, and at last stood up. He got ready, and was about to leave the ship's cabin. Then he smiled wryly, and returned to the shower.... In space, water was a precious substance. Since he had returned to Earth, he couldn't get used to such luxury: the daily uses of water, such as washing his face and rinsing his mouth. Then he went out onto the top deck.

There was no wind, and the mirror-like sea didn't have a single wrinkle. The pale sunlight of the dawn lay on the sea like mist, bathing it in a faint orange light.

He could hear the sound of the waves lapping the ship's side clearly, like breathing, but nothing else. The roar of the hydrofoil's reactor had also ceased.

Yūichi leaned forward over the railing, narrowed his eyes, and searched for the shape of Aphrodite: *It should be there.* For a while, he could only see the purple clouds trailing over the horizon; but at last, a tiny black speck floated into his field of vision, like the tip of a needle.

Aphrodite.

Yūichi blinked his eyes, automatically shading them with his hand, and stared at that black point.

The hydrofoil, with its reactor cut off, was coasting on inertia alone, at an irritatingly slow speed.

The first thing to take shape clearly was the flock of seagulls dancing over the ocean. A host of seagulls were flying, looping in varying arcs, circling lazily over the ocean. He couldn't hear their voices yet.

Even so, the gulls—he still couldn't hear them— looked as if they were dancing in time to some music.

Yūichi stared fixedly at the flock. They circled, in ever-larger circles. The flaring circle of a girl's skirt. The gulls circled tighter. The girl stands on her tiptoes, arches her back, claps her hands on top of her

2063 :: Age 30

head. *Forward three steps, two to the side; step, step; clap hands.*

From the horizon, the voice of the Aphrodite Kid came rising, echoing loudly in Yūichi's head. Making Anita's cheeks red, dancing at the Laugh Cat. Yūichi dancing too.

Anita shifting, spreading her arms as if flying. Yūichi bending over, stepping high, stamping down. *Turn, step, step* . . . In an instant, the reborn memories of Anita, together with the flock of seagulls, changed: turned to powder, broke like a mirror shattering, vanished.

Yūichi shut his eyes, tightly, and gripped the rail with all his might. He couldn't hear the voice of the Aphrodite Kid any more. He could only hear the monotonous refrain of the waves against the side of the ship. Yūichi opened his eyes, breathed out heavily. He whispered to himself, deep in his heart—*That's over fifty years ago* . . . He suddenly felt the presence of someone behind him, and slowly turned. The man named Crane was standing there. He was a 3D-TV news reporter: too thin, short, and a little balding. He was always smiling like he had been made a fool of, but in spite of that he talked aggressively to people—a mass-produced mass-media person.

"Brings back old memories, huh?" asked Crane in an over-familiar voice. "How long is it since you were on Aphrodite?"

"I wonder." Yūichi looked away from Crane: looked at the horizon. He still couldn't see Aphrodite. He stood staring at the horizon, and finally said in an amazed voice, "Thirty-five years . . ."

Of course, he didn't feel as if he were thirty-five years older. To him it was the same as if a 3D photo had been changed in a click, and thirty-five years had vanished with it. Physically, too, he was still, no mistake, thirty years old.

It happened to all the astronauts who traveled to the stars. Even though they logically understood the Urashima Effect, they couldn't truly grasp the gap between them and their counterparts on Earth. When they returned, they always became lost and disoriented in that difference. Yūichi was lost too.

"Thirty-five years, . . ." said Crane, shaking his head. "It's strange. And in spite of it, you're still thirty years old. Even though it's the same thirty-five years, it's been a long time for Aphrodite." A long, long time. While Yūichi had been on the starship for a year, Aphrodite had seen over thirty-four years. Thirty-five years . . . That was enough time, more than enough time, for a city to rust, to become deserted, and destined to be destroyed.

Still, could you believe it? That Aphrodite was going to be destroyed today. With its destruction, everything Yūichi valued, all his memories, would vanish from the world—Yūichi couldn't accept it. "Why are you following me around?" he asked, at last. "You're not likely to get a good story out of it."

"You star-traveling astronauts are heroes even now," said Crane bluntly. "You're always fascinating material for us mass-media people."

"I don't want to hear the usual society tributes." Yūichi shook his head, irritated. "I want to hear the truth."

"I see . . ."

Crane grinned and scratched the back of his neck. Then he pursed his lips a little, squinted as if thinking, and finally spoke softly. "The fact is, I don't totally agree with space development . . . How

2063 :: Age 30

do I say it . . . I can't help feeling that astronauts are people who can't adapt to reality. And when human society is pulled along by that group of non-adapters, I'm afraid."

Yūichi swung his gaze back to the horizon for a second time, silent. The orange light of morning had begun to spread along the horizon. He seemed to see an island, or was it an illusion?

"That's why I'm interested in you," continued Crane, not put off by the fact Yūichi had turned his back. "You gained the qualifications to ride starships with unusual speed. In less than a year, they say. They say you're a born astronaut . . . It's natural I'd have an interest, isn't it?"

"I'm not an astronaut, . . ." muttered Yūichi. "Just an engineer second-class."

"The public doesn't worry about that. They think all the people who fly starships are astronauts." Crane paused for a moment, and wet his lips. "When I heard you were going out especially to see Aphrodite's destruction, I thought it was a story. I don't know what memories you have of Aphrodite, but it certainly isn't ordinary to go see it on the ship dispatched by the UN to destroy it. It's more than sentimentality—maybe you're too far out of touch with reality.

"Maybe you're losing sight of reality. . . . Why did you decide to come watch Aphrodite?"

Yūichi didn't know.

Of course, it would be a lie to say that Yūichi didn't want to take one last look at Aphrodite before it was destroyed. And, true, he was sentimental. Whatever else, Aphrodite was the city where Yūichi spent the most emotional times of his life, from seventeen to twentyeight. Still, that wasn't the only thing that was making him return to Aphrodite. He felt there was another, more *real* reason. He didn't know what it was, but . . .

"I feel a little bad about saying all this in front of you. . . . I'm thinking of using you going to Aphrodite to draw out the fact that astronauts can't adapt to the reality we all share. . . . Don't get upset." Yūichi wasn't upset. He wasn't even listening to Crane's words. In fact, he wasn't even really there.

Yūichi extended his neck, clutched the rail, and stared forward, devouring the sight.

The morning sun dyed the horizon red, and cast spears of golden light to the sea, boldly lighting up the shape of an island. It was unmistakably Aphrodite.

▲

The hull of the ship rose over his head, blocking the sun and suddenly darkening the view.

The ship, looking as if it had been abandoned for years, was damaged by the tide and the wind—rotted—and the oozing moss overhanging it looked like dark green pus.

Of all the ships that had once packed the harbor of Herhip, it was the only one left. Yūichi felt again the weight of thirty-five years. His small craft circled the hulk, and soon the pier came rushing up before him.

Yūichi cut the throttle, and the craft drifted to the pier on inertia. The fine, crepe-like waves reflected the bright morning sun, bathing Yūichi in a shower of light.

With a small crunch, the craft's bottom bit into the pier. Yūichi fixed the craft nimbly, and pulled himself up to the top.

2063 :: Age 30

He looked at Herhip for the first time in thirty-five years. He hadn't expected to see anything else, but still he couldn't help being shocked at the total desolation that thirty-five years had brought to Herhip.

Replacing human beings, "destruction" and "decay" seemed to have settled in and thrived.

Moss closely overgrew the paving stones in Herhip, and the smell of rot was in the air. The stones themselves had jagged cracks running through them from the action of sun and surf.

Maze-like Herhip sector had been invaded by fierce growths of vegetation, and now looked like a deserted city in the jungle. Ivy crawled along the walls of a house about to collapse, weeds were sprouting profusely in the cracks in the paving stones, and ferns had sprouted in the narrow roads. Pots and frypans and such were strewn on the roads, further intensifying the desolation. Fleeing the encroachment of the invading plants, the spire of the church in Herhip looked like an arm reaching skyward, seeking help. In places, vividly colored flowers showed their petals; but even so, it was terribly depressing. Yūichi stood in dazed silence for a minute, then, shaking his head, began to walk slowly.

Aphrodite was scheduled for destruction tonight at seven o'clock. There were many reasons given for the destruction of Aphrodite—that it interfered with ocean currents, and that it affected fishing on the continental shelf—but none was very convincing. The fact was, Aphrodite had been used as a naval base by a certain nation, and the other countries had decided—through what tangled path of reasoning, no one knew—that the answer was destruction.

Thirty-five years was a long time, but it seemed it wasn't long enough to eliminate the root causes of conflicts between nations.

Yūichi had been allowed to land on Aphrodite after he had promised to return by six that evening. Of course, it had only been possible because he was an astronaut, with the full VIP treatment. If he had been a boat boy, like before, he would only gotten a flat refusal.

Crane had begged to accompany him, but Yūichi somehow managed to scrape him off and come alone. Yūichi himself didn't clearly understand why he had to come alone. Because he was soaked in sentimentalism, because he wanted to say goodbye to Aphrodite . . . Well, those were certainly true; but there was something else deep in his heart bothering him too. *It's more than sentimentality—maybe you're too far out of touch with reality. Maybe you're losing sight of reality* . . . Crane's words echoed in his head, painfully.

Yūichi climbed up the hillside road.

The collapsed houses, the road hidden by ferns, were corrected charitably in Yūichi's head, and came to overlay his memories. The proud, glorious Aphrodite floated up ghost-like from the desolation. As if he had a magic eye, Yūichi could see the old Aphrodite.

Yūichi finally crested the hill, avoiding puddles of water in the cracks in the pavement, and crushing the weeds. He stood there for a while.

It was the Laugh Cat.

He gave a small sigh, and entered the Laugh Cat. The door screeched a little louder than he

2063 :: Age 30

expected, and the dark smell of vegetation assailed him. Inside, vegetation flourished like it was in a greenhouse. Ferns crawled over the sofa, and hibiscus overflowed with blooms. An open hole in the wall let the strong sunlight in, and reinforced the image of a greenhouse. A bee slowly flew by, floating in the heat. The buzzing sounded strangely lazy, making him drowsy. The air was hot, rich, and glowed like melted butter. The thick aroma of wild roses drifted in the air.

Yūichi stood in the doorway, staring at the counter. The best wine of the Laugh Cat and two wineglasses were still there. It looked as if the last two people to leave had toasted the Laugh Cat.

Naturally, Yūichi knew who they had been. A familiar name rose to his throat.

But he couldn't say it now. Thirty-five years had passed—thirty five long years—and the fact that Yūichi was still only thirty years old had become a final barrier between him and other people, made him a dweller in another world.

Yūichi walked slowly to the counter, and picked up a wineglass. He ran his finger along the rim as if enjoying the feel—as if familiar people had come to life again through the glass.

Yūichi replaced the glass quietly, and turned to the jukebox in the corner.

It was overgrown with ivy, layered with white dust, and the picture on the body had faded away. Yūichi dropped a coin from his pocket into the slot. He searched for an Aphrodite Kid song and pressed the switch.

Of course, it didn't work. Dead silence.

Yūichi smiled a little, sadly, hit the jukebox lightly with his hand, and walked away. He could still hear the languid buzzing of the bee even after he left the Laugh Cat.

Yūichi strolled down the hill. The sunlight was blistering, and the smell of the plants was strong enough to choke him. The sun flamed, and from the top of the hill Aphrodite was as insubstantial as a city at the bottom of a fishbowl. He was drenched in sweat in an instant, the sweat dripping from his chin to leave black stains on the stones. Yūichi realized he had forgotten what it was like to be in the middle of the heat, moving, drenched in sweat. The hot sweat of astronaut training, the cold sweat of starflight, were different—this was the real thing, real sweat. Walking in the hot sunshine with sweat streaming down his body, Yūichi felt happy. Yūichi suddenly stopped, and cocked his head. He stared at a point in space. He could hear it!

Unquestionably, he could hear the Aphrodite Kid's voice! He could hear it, from far, far away, almost extinguished by the wind, but unmistakably. And Aphrodite was supposed to be deserted! Yūichi began to run with all his speed. He ran, stopping at intersections to listen for the song and check the direction, and ran again. He ran.

In the bright sunshine, through the tropical plants and the sun's radiance, he ran. It was as if the clock had turned backwards ten years, and his body was brimming with the vitality of an eighteen year old again. At last, almost kicking the door down, he burst into a certain house. He galloped up the stairs, and opened the door to the room at the end. A huge audio system occupied the entire wall. As Yūichi burst into the room, the recording

2063 :: Age 30

of the Aphrodite Kid was just ending. With a final sound like a sigh, the player fell silent. The player was probably powered by stored energy from some kind of solar cells. That it could still work wasn't particularly strange in itself. What was strange was who had turned it on. Yūichi stood in the deserted room, and listened to the wind gently whispering over the windowsill. A faint smell of pipe tobacco hung in the air.

▲▲▲▲ 2

Cestus Plaza hadn't changed that much.

There were no weeds, no cracks in the columns; desolation and destruction hadn't left their cruel scars yet.

It looked exactly the same as he remembered it. Still, it was different, somehow . . .

He couldn't grasp exactly what the difference was, but the wind that blew through the columns, and their blue silhouettes, all had a sense of disharmony. How to say it . . . It was as if it had lost its heart, its fundamental concept, and only the empty shape was left.

The lotus canopies of Cestus Plaza were open, and the furious rays of the sun rained down. The lines of the Doric columns rose up to the blank blue sky, reflecting the white sun.

Of course, the thermostats and the air curtains had long since died, and Cestus Plaza was stagnant with stifling heat.

The loud tread of his boots echoed amid the columns, becoming fainter and fainter, finally vanishing. The echo had a wretched ring, as if the heart had been torn out of it.

Yūichi walked through Cestus Plaza with an almost absentminded stride.

Setting foot in Aphrodite again, he couldn't help

but recall the events of the Twentieth Anniversary Festival. The difference between those glorious memories and the present Cestus Plaza was too huge, pushing him away from reality.

Now that he thought of it, the fact that the concept behind Cestus Plaza owed so much to the Greek temples of Cape Sounion was not a very good omen. Maybe Cestus Plaza had been doomed to become a ruin.

The columns of Cestus Plaza stood hushed, like eternal, taciturn giants. In the stagnant heat a slight odor of mold rose at their feet. The smell from the surface of the stepping stones—the thick, sweetish, sleepy smell of rank fungus—resembled the stench of death.

The sound of his footsteps echoed, vanishing silently into the blue sky. Finally, that echo—in Yūichi's head—became a voice. At first it was a whisper; then, like changing the volume on a speaker, it became clearer and clearer, changing to a roar of anger.

Do you have any idea? . . . A young boy's voice. *Do you understand where Aphrodite is now?* . . . He couldn't recall the boy's face. Over forty years ago. He would be much, much older than Yūichi now.

Like the roar of the surf, voices and sounds overflowed in Yūichi's head, quarrelling—angry voices; the dull thud of a punch landing; the sound of running feet; laughter . . . Three boys fleeing tangled together, in the shadows of the columns of Cestus Plaza. With black and blue faces, with blood streaming from their noses, but laughing together all the same, they ran. Gil, and Voight, and Yūichi . . .

Yūichi almost couldn't breathe for the vividness of those memories as they came flooding back. He

2063 :: Age 30

shut his eyes tightly, painfully, and stood rooted to the spot.

On the back of his eyelids, red and blue spots of light were scattered in the blackness. For a while, he could hear only the sound of blood pounding through his temples, and the wind slipping through the columns—then the memories faded, and he felt the sadness of being the only person there.

When he first heard it, he thought it was an illusion.

When he heard it the second time, he could clearly tell it was the sound of real footsteps, and not an illusion.

In Cestus Plaza, Aphrodite—where nobody was supposed to be living—he could hear the sound of somebody walking in sandals.

Yūichi opened his eyes, and looked around.

He saw something move out of the corner of his eye. Partly hidden by the columns, he couldn't clearly see it, but it was obviously somebody running out of Cestus Plaza.

The cork heels of the sandals sounded loudly for a moment against the stones.

Automatically, Yūichi began to run too.

He knew he had to tell that person, whoever it was, that Aphrodite was to be destroyed tonight at seven o'clock; but more than that, more than anything, he was possessed by his memories, and simply had to run—he had forgotten himself completely.

The heat waves rising from the stones of Cestus Plaza turned the fleeing figure into a shimmering mirage. The ever-receding ripples of a mirage seemed to make the figure vanish every so often, frightening Yūichi.

Running, he cut across Cestus Plaza. The other

figure kept fleeing, up the ramp and onto the elevated Electronic Control Highway.

Yūichi followed after, rushing up the ramp in a single burst, and felt the ground shudder beneath him.

Yūichi instantly grabbed the guardrail, and waited for the vibration to stop. The shaking wasn't severe enough to make him feel in danger. Like it was boiling from below, he felt the concrete beneath his feet shake. The image of Herself sector, spread out beyond the Electronic Control Highway, doubled and tripled like an out-of-focus 3D-TV picture, in need of fine-tuning.

He heard the sound of shattering glass from somewhere.

It was like the rocking of a fishing boat in a squall, and it was a familiar shaking. The sense of fond remembrance was even stronger than the fear.

The shaking faded, and he finally couldn't feel it under his feet at all. Herself was no longer blurring, either.

Yūichi breathed a sigh, and released the guardrail.

Then, for the first time, he noticed that a young girl was standing in front of him.

"The giant whirlpool," said the young girl, in a relaxed tone. "Before, Aphrodite almost never shook. . . . It's getting steadily worse."

"I thought so," nodded Yūichi, and then asked after a short pause, "Why did you run away?"

"Because you were chasing me," she said calmly.

"But of course!" Yūichi couldn't help but give a wry smile. It made sense.

A very odd girl. A little thin, and as tall as Yūichi. Her hair and eyes were black—big, beautiful eyes—

2063 :: Age 30

and maybe because of it, she had a very exotic look. She was maybe a quarter Asian. In a loose summer sweater, she looked like a street child. She may not have been beautiful in the strict sense, but she certainly was striking.

"What are you doing here, mister?" she asked in her unconcerned voice.

Yūichi smiled again. First because he had been called *mister*, and then because he had been planning to ask her the same thing. He felt she had outmaneuvered him somehow.

"Not doing anything," he said. "Just walking around Aphrodite."

"Well, then, will you help me a little?"

"With what?"

"It's not that difficult," she waved to him to come along, turned her back to him, and began to walk briskly along the Electronic Control Highway.

Yūichi had no choice but to follow her.

Why are you living in Aphrodite, a city that's supposed to be deserted? ... The question came to his lips, but somehow she had an air about her that made him hesitate.

Maybe it was because she made him think of the first time he had met Anita. They had nothing in common, but somehow they were paired in Yūichi's head—maybe because Anita, when had they first met, had been exactly this age.

In any case, he had to tell her that Aphrodite was scheduled for destruction tonight. He could hardly let her be killed by his omission. Naturally—but not now. It would be no trouble to tell her, for example, an hour from now.

Yūichi felt like enjoying a talk with that strange girl for a while. The Electronic Control Highway was dry like a desert. Heat rose, and it was covered in a thick layer of white dust. In front of them, electronic cars lay deserted, rusted, and eaten by the weather. It was like the Elephant's Graveyard.

She stopped in front of one car, and said "Will you push this with me?"

He looked at the car.

It was an ordinary EV. It looked no better than any of the other cars. Scrap. Of course, there was no energy stored up, and even if there was a little charge in the battery it was absurd to expect it to move even a centimeter.

"What do you want to do?" Yūichi asked in a confused voice. "The electronic system is totally useless, and driving on manual is out of the question. It won't drive...."

"I don't want to drive it," she said, walking to rear of the car, putting both hands on the bumper and looking at Yūichi.

Yūichi paused, shrugged as if giving in, and then put his hands on the car's body in line with the girl's.

They both pushed. With a squealing the car began to move.

Pushing the car wasn't such hard work in itself, but the sun was close to zenith.

They were both drenched in sweat.

The two of them pushed the car in silence over the Electronic Control Highway connecting Herhip and Herself, over the sea spreading out around them.

To Yūichi, the Electronic Control Highway—elevated above the sea, with no cars at all driving by—was an unreal scene.

The white highway ran straight along the blue sea with nothing to contrast it with. That simple, clear

2063 :: Age 30

color scheme was bent and distorted by the tsunami of rising heat waves, like looking through distorted glass.

The incessant heat has opened pits in the surface of the highway, like craters in hard bread. An ugly highway littered with deserted cars: a scene after a nuclear war.

Everything was burned under the sizzling sun, nothing could be cleaner. Only the playful monotone of the sea, and the crying of the wheeling gulls.

Screech, screech... The car squealed again, a wail.

In the blazing sun, with a waterfall of sweat cascading down, it was too much trouble to talk. While pushing the car together with the girl, he felt a loneliness as if they were the last survivors of an extinct world. He knew he was thinking that way because Aphrodite was scheduled for destruction tonight, and he was getting sentimental.... "This is fine," she said, stopping and wiping the sweat from her forehead with her fist.

This place didn't look especially different. Only, probably as the result of some accident, the guardrail was twisted and a large gap lay open.

The girl pulled her lip between her finger and thumb as if thinking, then picked up a large stone from near her feet. She raised it up above her head, and threw it down on the car with all her force.

The front glass of the car shattered into powder.

The girl, breathing heavily, turned to the surprised Yūichi and said "Smash the rear glass, would'ya?"

"Why?"

"You'll see."

Yūichi shrugged, picked up a rock as she had, and went around to the rear of the car. He had followed her directions this far. If he turned away now, he wouldn't get a chance to talk to her—and he did feel a bit of excitement at smashing a car window with a rock.

After the rear window shattered, he turned to her, and asked in a slightly cynical voice "Well, what's next?"

"We push again," she answered. "We push the car into the sea."

Yūichi obeyed promptly. He had no special interest in thinking about her actions logically. He suspected he wasn't likely to understand anyway.

They both went to the back of the car again, and pushed together. The front wheels pushed out through the gap in the guardrail, the car balanced like a seesaw for a moment, and then plummeted into the sea.

It was exactly like a slow-motion film. They could hear almost no sound when it hit the water—the car floated upside down for about ten seconds, then sank with a huge gurgling of bubbles. Really, quite disappointing.

They were both breathing raggedly, and were too busy mopping sweat to feel like talking.

"I guess you'll tell me now," said Yūichi at last. "Why in the world did we do that?"

"The car will make a good breeding place for fish," she said, shrugging her shoulders a little. "Then we can fish for them."

It wasn't that surprising when he heard it. A car with its windows smashed would be a great spot for fish. A superb plan—but more than the plan, he was interested that she had used the word we.

"So other people live on Aphrodite too?"

"Of course. People can't live alone."

2063 :: Age 30

"About how many?"

"Well, I've never really counted..." As if it were a habit, she pulled her lip again with her fingers in thought, then said "Over a hundred. Maybe a lot more."

That was, to say the least, quite unexpected. The official announcement said Aphrodite had been uninhabited for years now—if it were inhabited, they would have to rethink the plan to destroy it. It would take a lot of preparation to evacuate a hundred people. It was certainly impossible in one night.

"Who are you people?" asked Yūichi, in a slightly unbelieving voice. "Don't you know that it's been forbidden to enter Aphrodite for years now?"

She bounced her shoulders. Of course she knew, just didn't worry about it.

"We're companions," she said. "I can't really explain who we are. There are lots of people here, but we're all companions."

"Will you introduce me to everybody?"

"Sure," she nodded. She took a rolled-up cloth from her pocket, unwrapped a pipe, and tamped tobacco into it. When she bit on the pipe, she lit it with a practiced hand, and breathed out the smoke as if it were delicious—Yūichi remembered that pipe's smell.

"So it was you," he said, "You were listening to the Aphrodite Kid's tape a little while ago."

"Yeah, I listen a lot."

"You like the Kid's songs?"

"Yeah. Lots," she said, and, taking the pipe from her mouth, looked at Yūichi appraisingly. "Mister, were you a Kid fan?"

"I was in love with him."

"Mm, . . ." she said, and puffed once, twice. "Mister, before I introduce you to everybody, let me introduce you to the Aphrodite Kid."

". . ."

"Not interested?"

"Of all the . . . crazy, . . ." mumbled Yūichi in a hoarse voice. "The Aphrodite Kid can't still be here."

"Come on, you'll see." She laughed like a playful little girl, and, turning her back on Yūichi again, strode off.

"Hey! Wait!" Yūichi called agitated. "It's hard to talk. What's your name?"

"Anita," she turned and said. Then her eyes grew big. "What's wrong? Why do you look so astonished?"

"Nothing." Yūichi shook his head with a smile. "I used to know a girl with the same name."

It was nothing. He used to know a girl with the same name. Only that . . .

3

Maybe it was a little strange for someone who'd lived here so long, but Yūichi had never set foot in either the Control Tower or the Information Tower at the control complex.

The complex hadn't been off-limits to the general public; in fact, it had been included in the tour.

If he had felt like going, he could have gone at any time. He never had, though, maybe because it was just too close.

To a young man who had spent the most blessed, rich years of his life in Aphrodite, from seventeen to twenty-eight, the Center just wasn't that interesting. To any normal boy, the ocean or girls or something else were always far more compelling.

So Yūichi, returning to Aphrodite after thirty-five years, was entering the Information Tower for the first time. He felt a little daunted, but that wasn't too strange.

Anita, naturally, jauntily entered the tower without noticing his feelings. It was probably impossible for her to be daunted by anything.

The floor was remarkably polished. It didn't shine, but the walls hadn't fallen, and there was no sign of rats scurrying about. It felt like it could start operation again tomorrow morning if you just sent the right people.

The scars left by thirty-five years of time were still present, though. It was empty of people, true, but the emptiness was different from that of a holiday or weekend. The electricity and lights were off; but also the vitality, the thing that warmed your soul, was missing—however well-preserved, a deserted ruin was a deserted ruin.

Entering the Information Tower, Anita went straight to the basement.

The elevator was dead, of course, so they used the emergency stairs. The emergency stairs were seemingly endless, and over-thirty Yūichi began to get worn-out.

Yūichi, with his jaw set and breathing raggedly, kept thinking what she could have meant by saying she would introduce him to the Aphrodite Kid.

He couldn't figure it out.

At the bottom of the stairs was a huge steel door.

Anita pushed the door with both hands, and it slowly opened with a rusty protest. If the Information Center had still been functioning, it would have opened smoothly on hydraulics.

The confined heat steamed into his face. The odor of mold was strong. There were some windows to the outside, and the room was brighter than he expected, but it still took him some time to get used to the light.

As his eyes adjusted, a huge green display screen slowly floated up from the bottom of the darkness. Darkly glimmering control consoles were grouped around the display screen.

It was a computer room, but he doubted it would ever work again even with power, due to the heat. It was nothing more than a mountain of steel, of scrap metal.

2063 :: Age 30

Yūichi stood for a while, staring at the computer room.

Dust was piled deeply over everything. There were no crumbling walls, and no sprouting weeds; but he still felt, for some reason, that the desolation here was even more intense than what he had felt in the Laugh Cat or Cestus Plaza.

Animals were not the only things to lose their body heat and slowly rot away when they died.

Yūichi turned his head around slowly, resting his eyes on Anita, who was sitting at the control panel.

"This is the Aphrodite Kid?" he asked. "You're saying that this computer is him?"

"That's right," nodded Anita guilelessly. "The Aphrodite Kid never was a real person. There were some talented singers, but their voices were combined into a good-feeling, heart-warming voice by this computer. It analyzed what type of song the people wanted to hear, and then composed it."

He could tell she didn't intend to hurt him. Probably, she felt bad about Yūichi worshiping the Aphrodite Kid without knowing the truth. Maybe she even felt a kind of righteous indignation.

Even so, Yūichi couldn't help but feel a bit angry. Some things you're being better off never knowing.

Now that he thought about it, he realized the Kid's songs had always been with him and his group. When he danced with that Anita the first time at the Laugh Cat, the jukebox had been playing the Kid.

He was the symbol of Aphrodite City; in a way, a symbol of adolescence for Yūichi and his friends. If the Kid had been only a virtual presence—that would be to say that Yūichi's youth itself had been based on a lie, wouldn't it?

For an instant, he was possessed by the sadness of feeling sand run through his fingers.

He knew without a doubt, without even asking, that the person who had created the Aphrodite Kid had been Mr. Caan.

There was no question that Mr. Caan had felt it absolutely necessary for a singer to act as the symbol of Aphrodite, to bind the people together even more strongly. It was something he would have thought of.

It hurt to realize just how much Mr. Caan had loved Aphrodite. To protect his creation, Mr. Caan had accepted any deception, and hadn't been afraid to smear mud on his own reputation, or to have secret dealings with the major powers.

And it was all because he had loved Aphrodite. To Mr. Caan, Aphrodite was right, was the ideal. As long as Aphrodite existed, all sins would be forgiven, all corrected—and certainly, Aphrodite had sprouted the first germ of that ideal society, and had been an experiment worth continuing.

But, Mr. Caan had failed. No, not only Mr. Caan had failed: he had to say that Yūichi, that Voight, that Gil, that everybody living in Aphrodite had failed. And it had been an experiment that shouldn't have failed....

"How do you know this computer was the Aphrodite Kid?" asked Yūichi, steeling himself against painful thoughts.

"One of the guys is hot on computers," said Anita, in her innocent voice. "He searched the data, and found out."

"I see...." As he nodded, a squeal sounded from the steel door behind him.

Yūichi turned, and saw three youngsters standing there.

2063 :: Age 30

They were maybe seventeen or eighteen, and had a slightly grungy look to them. All three looked pretty bright, but their faces held an attitude of hostility to Yūichi.

"Anita," said one, in a strained voice, "Don't say anything else to that guy."

"Why?" Anita asked, a little at a loss.

"A boat came to Aphrodite. They're going to blow it up. He's one of them."

Anita looked at Yūichi's face, astonished. Yūichi had no defense: it was true.

"You, come with us," they said, as if talking to a criminal they were taking away.

Herleg had changed in thirty-five years, but it wasn't desolate. Quite the opposite.

Houses lined the terraced slope, just like before, but most of them had been rebuilt into either solar houses or vinyl-roofed aquaculture tanks. The slopes themselves had become fields, or turned into pastures for grazing cows. Free-ranging chickens dotted the landscape here and there.

Most of the men and women working there were in their teens, and most of the boys had long hair and beards, making him think of a Mormon town. Still, there wasn't the oppressive atmosphere a strict religious community would have.

Just as before, since Herleg was built on the hills, the sun was fierce and hot, and clean. Under that sunlight, the sweat-drenched shapes of the laboring youngsters were refreshing, emotionally moving.

More than that, though, he was noticing that the youngsters were standing, and following him, like a criminal. One after another, they stopped their work and got into line behind him, shuffling along as if escorting a criminal to the gallows. . . . Yūichi couldn't suppress the image.

Pushed and prodded from behind, he was still mute. What they had to say to each other was just too different. Aphrodite was supposed to be uninhabited, so where had all these people popped up from? He couldn't believe his eyes in spite of the fact they were all around him. Yūichi was pushed along the walkway to the boat harbor, and ordered to stop in front of one of the boathouses.

He stared at the sea for a moment, vaguely, then noticed that it was his old workplace—Mr. Caan's boathouse—and was astonished.

Mr. Caan's boathouse was etched deeply into Yūichi's memory, and had become almost a private myth to him, so that even when he actually returned to it, he couldn't believe it was real. How much he loved this place, was proud of it . . .

At the unexpected shock, his nervous balance suddenly shattered, and Yūichi felt himself crying.

He turned his face away, and began to rub his eyes with his fists. The youngsters peered at him from the sides, as if he were a most peculiar thing.

Suddenly, he heard bubbles boiling up in the water. To Yūichi it was a familiar sound, a well-loved one.

Yūichi raised his eyes, and saw there was a single submersible rising up to the surface.

For an instant, it looked like the *Rosebud* to Yūichi's trembling eyes.

Of course, it wasn't. The *Rosebud* of decades ago would hardly be moving after all that time.

That submersible didn't look much better than scrap, but it was still a much newer model than the *Rosebud* had been.

2063 :: Age 30

It advanced quietly, and drifted sideways precisely to the pier. Superb piloting.

The hatch opened, and a single young man lightly jumped to the pier.

His straw-colored hair was held by a hair-band, and he looked clever but somehow introspective. His beard was neatly trimmed, but if he let it grow, he might resemble Christ, he was so painfully thin.

"I'm Chris," he said briskly, and stuck out his right hand to Yūichi. "I'm sort of the acting leader here. Glad to meet you."

Yūichi mumbled his own name, and shook hands. He couldn't decide if he was being treated as a prisoner or received as a guest.

"Have a seat," said Chris, and sat down on the edge of the pier, dangling his long legs. He took an avocado from his pants pocket, and, holding it on one hand like a plate, he took a knife from his rear pocket with the other, cutting it neatly in two. He gave half to Yūichi, sitting next to him on the pier.

"Have some?" Yūichi thanked him, took the avocado, and ate the ripe green flesh. A rich vegetable smell rose, and he felt the nutritious fat spreading through his mouth—sitting in the breeze, eating an avocado this way, he felt as if he were once again eighteen years old.

"We eat lots of avocados," said Chris. "Here, we don't lack much, at least when it comes to avocados."

"It didn't used to be the same," said Yūichi, wiping his mouth with the back of his hand. "I think they used to be imported from out around Hawaii."

"They used to—the people in power in Aphrodite then didn't worry much about food self-sufficiency.

They thought that as long as the ocean resources were developed well, that other countries would continue to supply them."

"And you don't think that way."

"We don't," said Chris, shaking his head. "We feel that for a floating city like Aphrodite, food self-sufficiency is a basic need, to avoid being dependent on the major powers."

"You figure you'll go it alone."

"Right."

"Who are you all?" asked Yūichi, changing topics. "Where did you all come from?"

Chris was silent a minute, industriously licking the avocado flesh from his fingers. His eyes had the look that said they were calculating just how much it was safe to tell.

"We came here from many different countries, . . ." he said at last.

"None of us liked having our lives planned out from birth to death; we felt suffocated, oppressed, and escaped from our old countries.

"Without any special reasons, we just ended up gathering here in Aphrodite."

"The *why* is pretty vague."

"I might be the leader, but my authority doesn't extend to asking what they were thinking when they came here. And even if it did, I wouldn't ask."

Chris folded his hands into a triangle in front of his face and spoke almost as if chanting. Under the shadow of his hands, he was staring at the sea.

"For me, I was raised hearing about Aphrodite. In Aphrodite there is freedom, real freedom, I heard. I believed that if I only went to Aphrodite, then everything would be OK . . . One day, when I was

2063 :: Age 30

taking a occupational suitability test, I discovered I hated it all, and ran away."

It was a story Yūichi well understood. Even though his story was decades old, it was still the same.

"And?" asked Yūichi. "Are you satisfied with Aphrodite?"

"Aphrodite is desolation: nothing more, nothing less, . . ." smiled Chris. "I was naive. I should have noticed much earlier that you don't get anything for free. If you want to live in a free country, you have to build it yourself."

Yūichi sat watching the waves ebb and flow among the pilings. Finally, in a subdued voice, he said "It's not easy, Aphrodite has already failed once. . . ."

"We won't fail," said Chris, with determination. "We won't be hurried, we won't be afraid. We won't lose hope, but we also won't hold empty hope. We will not fail. Still . . ."

"Still?"

"We have no way to protect ourselves against attack from the outside. For example, if Aphrodite should be destroyed, we can't do a thing about it."

"How did you know?"

"Picked it up on the radio, . . ." said Chris. "I told them by radio that there are over a hundred people living here on Aphrodite, but of course they don't recognize us. They're all hard-assed bureaucratic types. They ordered us to leave Aphrodite at once. . . . We refused, naturally. I told them that if they tried to make us leave by force, we couldn't guarantee the life of the hostage in our care. . . ."

Yūichi looked at Chris' face for a while, then smiled bitterly and said as if talking to himself, "Of course. Makes perfect sense. . . ."

"I hereby place you under arrest," said Chris,

slowly standing up. He spoke regretfully. "We won't use any violence at all, so rest at ease."

"Thanks so much for your kindness,..." he replied cynically, but Chris had already left the pier.

In his place, the three boys approached Yūichi.

▲

Yūichi curled, motionless, on the floor.

The room looked as if it had been a storeroom: narrow, no furniture, the walls still naked pre-fab. It did have a window; but it was small, and had steel bars, and he couldn't see outside very well due to the thick grime on it.

The rays of the western sun pierced in through the window, firing the room into orange, and heating it into an almost unbearable steam bath.

In a word, it was unpleasant. Chris had promised not to use any violence, but locking a prisoner in this room sure felt like violence to him.

Yūichi felt as if he were submerged in hot water. His skin shone through his drenched shirt, and black spots of sweat plopped to the concrete.

But Yūichi didn't move. He sat with his knees up, arms crossed on top, and his face buried in his arms. He was totally motionless.

Yūichi was wondering *Why? Why he had come back to Aphrodite?*

Yūichi thought he was a sentimental person. Even so, he couldn't believe he had returned to Aphrodite just to satisfy his sentimentality. It wasn't clear even to himself, but there had to be another reason.

He had been thinking about it continuously, but hadn't been able to figure it out. Until now.

He thought he had finally worked it out, that he

2063 :: Age 30

knew now what he wanted to do, that he had finally grasped exactly what he had come to Aphrodite for.

But by the time he figured it out, though, he was a prisoner, and couldn't go where he had to.

Suddenly he raised his head, and stared at a point in space.

A single moth was fluttering around the window frame, as if beating it lightly. It wanted to escape to the outside; but it couldn't, because of the glass obstructing it. It was stupid confusion, the moth just beating itself against the window glass.

Yūichi reached through the bars, and opened up the window.

In Yūichi's eyes, looking after the escaped moth, was the glint of a strange brightness.

From behind him came the sound of the lock opening. Yūichi turned, and saw Anita watching him.

Anita looked confused somehow, as if she was feeling guilty.

"Something?" asked Yūichi in a level voice.

"I felt bad," Anita said, combing her long hair with both hands behind her head. "It's like it's somehow my fault you got taken, and I can't relax."

"It's not your fault."

"I think so too. But if anything happens to you, I'd feel really bad."

Yūichi looked at her face again. He felt his heart grow a little lighter.

"You'll help me?"

"The guard's gone to eat. You can leave here whenever you want to."

"If I do, will you be OK?"

"They won't ever know," Anita said, shrugging. "And even if they do, no one will get really angry.

Everybody thinks I'm just a girl who doesn't know what she's doing."

Yūichi gave a short laugh, then his face grew serious. "Will you do something for me?"

"If you're going to ask me to run away with you, don't. No chance."

"That's too bad . . ." Yūichi spoke from his heart, then continued. "I'm not running away either. When you see Chris, tell him I'm waiting in the Control Tower."

Anita looked at him dubiously but nodded strongly.

"Please?"

Yūichi slipped around her, and went outside.

The sunlight hadn't grown any weaker, but twilight seemed to be coming, and a breeze had started to blow from the sea. Looking down from near the top of the hills, Herleg was dyed in a pale gold color.

Yūichi stood looking for a while down at Herleg, then turned as he made a decision.

This was probably the last time he would ever see Herleg.

▲

The Control Tower was dark, damp, and smelled of rot. It was different from the excellent preservation of the Information Tower . . . too different. The Control Tower structure, the very walls, were dissolving, rotting from the inside.

He didn't know why.

Maybe when they learned that Aphrodite was to be sunk, the people working here had destroyed things on purpose.

2063 :: Age 30

If so, they had loved Aphrodite as much as—no more than—Yūichi did.

Yūichi was working in the Motive Power Room.

The western light seeping in the small window was his only aid, and when he was doing delicate work, his eyes hurt painfully.

He could stand that, but he was furious at tripping countless times over monkey wrenches and fuel cubes scattered across the floor. His fingers ached with cuts and bruises.

Yūichi disassembled the generator, cleaned the parts, and lubed it up well. It took far too much time, but he carefully checked every connection, and soldered the faulty ones until it was perfect.

When he had finally finished repairing and adjusting the generator, the Motive Power Room was almost pitch black, and he couldn't even see his feet. His hands floated white in the darkness.

He was worn out, but he didn't have time to rest. In another thirty minutes, the room would be sealed by the curtain of darkness, and he would be unable to see even his hands.

Yūichi slid his feet across the floor to the power distribution board.

It, too, looked like it needed a thorough checkout and soldering. He sighed at the thought.

When Yūichi was crouched under the distribution board, a brilliant light shone on him from behind.

Yūichi turned, and automatically put his hands over his eyes. "Chris?" he asked.

"Yeah, . . ." answered the holder of the light. "What are you doing here, if I may ask?"

"You came at just the right time. I have to check out the reactor and the control computer. It'd be a big help if you'd give me a hand. . . ."

"I asked what you're doing," said Chris, strongly.

"Don't worry," laughed Yūichi. "I'm going to explain now."

▲▲▲▲ 4

The sea was calm.

The black, deep sea was dyed with a faint blue light, and the tide roared in the distance.

The full moon was reflected on the sea, and like a gold pendant swaying on a girl's breast, it was scattered again and again by the passing waves.

Far away, floating like a jellyfish of light, was the brilliance of the hydrofoil. No doubt the captain and crew were raising a fuss with Yūichi held hostage.

Yūichi sat on the coast of Herself, watching the sea. He had thrown away his shirt, black with grease and sweat, and was dressed only in his jeans.

Yūichi's face was relaxed, a little absent.

His eyes seemed to be watching the sea, but in fact they were seeing something else entirely.

Unconsciously, Yūichi was grabbing fistfuls of sand, and scattering them into the wind, again and again.

Why?

Yūichi had simply needed to be alone, to watch the sea alone.

His ten years in Aphrodite, his time after that as an astronaut, all seemed to be nothing more than a dream when he watched the sea like this.

Had anything really changed, he wondered . . .

Suddenly, Yūichi recalled he had spent his youth sitting here, watching the sea, wondering what he would be doing in five years, in ten years.

When had that been?

He thought about it, but he couldn't recall.

A sadness that he had lost something very, very important sank into Yūichi's heart.

He jumped up, as if to shake something off, and ran towards the waves with all his heart. He dashed in, dressed as he was, and dove into the crashing surf head first.

Sinking, floating, Yūichi swam towards the harbor.

The water wasn't too cold, or even lukewarm, but just perfectly delicious.

Yūichi swam.

Yūichi couldn't imagine a greater joy than swimming—the pain in his arms, the tension in his calves.

He could see nothing but black spray and white foam. What he could hear was only his hard breathing.

Breathe, hold, stroke, kick . . . Yūichi was swimming with all his heart. He swam.

Finally, he tired, and stopped. He floated on the waves face-up, and waited for his ragged breathing to calm down. The sound of the waves came back to life.

He changed his course, and began to swim slowly, this time, back towards the coast. Herhip and Herself were both sunken in the darkness. Only in Herleg was there a little light scattered about.

Yūichi felt possessed by the desire to return there. A crazy desire to return, and to do it again, right . . .

But that was asking too much. Yūichi's generation had failed.

2063 :: Age 30

He didn't know why they had failed. In spite of the fact they shouldn't have, they couldn't have ... they had.

And now a new generation of youngsters was fighting with Aphrodite, choosing their own path to follow.

Yūichi couldn't go home again.

A person who has failed once, and left Aphrodite, can never return again.

When Yūichi finally struggled to shore, Chris was waiting.

The submersible was moored next to the jutting pier, quietly riding up and down.

"I wondered where you had gone," called Chris.

"What's the decision?" asked Yūichi, breathing hard.

"Everyone agreed with your plan. A few people weren't very happy, but at last, it's the only way.... We can't accept being forced off Aphrodite, and seeing it blown up."

"That's good," nodded Yūichi, and collapsed onto the sand as if his strings had been cut. He waited for his breathing to settle down, then looked up and asked, "Did you bring what I asked for?"

"Yeah, the super-inker was easy; but the other was a whole lot of trouble. Luckily, one of us is a pro, and managed to make one somehow ... We've got a little of almost everything in Aphrodite."

"Powerful?"

"Very powerful."

"Good," nodded Yūichi. "Teach me how to use it."

After a five-minute lecture, Yūichi had mastered it. It was simple enough that a child could have used it.

He picked up the super-inker and walked

towards the submersible. The super-inker was a cross between a paint sprayer and a paint-brush, and could write on anything. It used super-fast-drying ink.

Yūichi lay down on the pier, and skillfully drew something on the submersible's tail. Then he looked up at Chris, who was peering down with curiosity, and asked "What is it?"

"A flower."

Chris wrinkled his forehead. Obviously, he couldn't fathom Yūichi's actions.

"It's a rosebud," smiled Yūichi. "This ship is the *Rosebud*."

"A good luck charm?"

"Well, yeah, sort of . . ." Yūichi stood up, and nimbly jumped to the submersible. He finished the preparations quickly, and turned to the hatch.

"Say, when this is all over, why don't you stay here with us?" called Chris. "You're old, but you seem to be one of our side."

Yūichi froze for a moment with his hands on the hatch, then said in a queerly strained, low voice, "No, I'm already one of their side."

Chris waved his hand a little, and Yūichi's figure vanished into the submersible.

▲

He wasn't used to the submersible, so he was a little confused at first.

Still, it was basically the same type as the *Rosebud*, and he managed to check the main ballast tank, trim tanks, and propulsion system. Altering the angle of the variable thruster, then checking the video camera last seemed to be a habit with him.

2063 :: Age 30

Yūichi realized how long it had been since he had been in a submersible, and was a little surprised.

Subjectively, it was only a few years, but in the real world, it was decades ago.

He couldn't tell which was real.

Sitting in the control seat of the submersible like this, he felt he was still that same boat boy.

Probably—no, almost certainly—Mr. Caan was no longer in this world.

There was a blank in what he had thought, had felt, for years and tens of years. There was a little piloting technique left in Yūichi, but he knew he couldn't trust it.

He slowly submerged.

At fifty meters he used the control thrusters to come to a dead stop.

There was no problem with the controls, and the balance of weight and buoyancy was being controlled perfectly.

Yūichi smiled broadly, and pulled the main engine lever. Then it happened.

Countless bubbles burst across the screen like something had exploded. A loud clang sounded from below, and the submersible lost its balance for an instant. The hull screamed and squealed, and the pilot lamps flickered painfully.

Yūichi almost smashed his head into the instrument panel, catching himself just in time. He could imagine what would happen if he hit his head right now . . .

He felt the prow lift, and the submersible roll over. Once, twice, three times . . . Foul stomach fluids sluiced through his mouth.

He knew exactly what had happened. It was the giant whirlpool.

Yūichi reached out to blow all the water from the ballast tank at once, and surface, but his hand instead pulled the main engine propulsion lever with full force.

The rocket engines gave a mighty roar, and the submersible pierced forward into the giant vortex.

Yūichi himself couldn't explain his action—he had acted almost unconsciously. No, not quite.

Yūichi realized he was going to fight with the giant whirlpool. He didn't feel it was stupid. No, maybe it was stupid, but he had to fight. This time he wouldn't run away.

He was possessed by rage, that this whirlpool was the source of all the evil that had rotted Aphrodite, that now was trying to sink it, the thing that had broken Yūichi, and Voight, and Mr. Caan.

It was an illogical, baseless anger, but to him that whirlpool was something trying to destroy Aphrodite.

He couldn't run away.

This was vengeance.

Yūichi clenched his teeth, and clutched the propulsion lever.

The submersible burst into the giant whirlpool's crashing tumult. Not in a straight line, of course, but on a wildly weaving course. Somehow, he didn't know how, he didn't lose control.

The control thrusters were now almost useless. It was all he could do to stop from being punched about by wild, erratic currents, let alone think of controlling his course. If he hadn't been helped by shifting buoyancy, he would have lost control completely.

The screaming of the structural walls grew worse and worse. The danger lamps lit, and the metallic

2063 :: Age 30

shrieks of warning sirens sounded. The lights inside the cabin flickered as if panicked.

Scared.

Adrenaline from his fear was coursing through his body. He felt his temple convulsing in a tic. His throat was dry, and felt on fire. His hyper-tensed nerves felt like they were going to snap in two.

Yūichi made no effort to take his hand from the propulsion lever. Absolutely not.

The monitor was full of white bubbles like it was boiling. His vision was close to zero. Still, Yūichi's eyes bored into the monitor. It was his only hope.

A huge shadow came rushing towards him. One of Aphrodite's floating foundations. *Dive the submersible.* A straight shadow passed by the corner of his eye. One of Aphrodite's open waterways. *Bank the submersible. . . . repeat, repeat, repeat.*

The fear that his luck would run out clogged his throat. The feeling that he would miss a waterway or ram a foundation grabbed his heart.

I'm scared. Scared. So scared I want to vomit, I want to cry. . . .

Just then, like a miracle, the sea stilled around him, and the monitor showed it clearly: a gigantic chain. . . .

The sea cleared for only a moment, but it was plenty for Yūichi.

Yūichi grabbed the manipulator controls. He wasn't scared any more. He didn't feel anything. He didn't think anything.

The manipulator began to move. It was sinuous, like some boneless denizen of the deep. The computer-controlled, human-jointed arm had all the delicacy of a person's hand and fingers, and more.

The manipulator bent into a shape like a human

index finger, and flicked off the switch on the bomb it carried.

It was the bomb Chris and his group had managed to make. He still didn't know if it really had the power Chris said it had.

The manipulator tossed the bomb in an underhand throw. He blew all the ballast, rising at full speed.

Five seconds, ten seconds... Yūichi watched the monitor with blood-shot eyes. Greasy sweat smeared his forehead. He had begun praying, unconsciously. He kept praying.

Suddenly, a fierce light bloomed on the Monitor.

He let forth a shout of joy. Through the dark sand-smoke, he could clearly see the thick chain floating, broken. Aphrodite was free!

Of course, Aphrodite hadn't been anchored by it. It was impossible to absorb Aphrodite's motion energy with ten chains, or a hundred.

Not by brute force, but rather by using a dynamic positioning system: a huge rudder and impeller to exactly balance the forces of the currents, and the tide, and the wind.

The signaling device was planted on the sea floor, and the Control Tower had controlled everything from the signals it sent. But when Aphrodite became uninhabited—and it had been truly uninhabited, at one time—they had been forced to change.

The UN, afraid of Aphrodite drifting, tried to anchor this floating city by force.

For financial and technical reasons, they used the weight of the chains themselves, like a sort of ocean-anchor. And with the idea of concentrating that energy, they had gathered them all into a single giant chain.

2063 :: Age 30

Yūichi had figured that if he could just remove that one chain, then Aphrodite would be able to move again. They had no time to slowly wind up the chain, because Aphrodite might be destroyed even tonight.... Blowing up the chain was the only option left.

There would be no problem stopping Aphrodite later. Just start up the dynamic positioning system again, and that would solve it.

He didn't know yet if Aphrodite had become mobile again or not.

Yūichi, though, was sure that he had won his battle.

The submersible was still being thrown about by the giant whirlpool, but he no longer worried about it.

He was too busy laughing.

He was too busy laughing real laughter, bursting up from deep inside, shaking his whole body.

The giant shadow of Aphrodite was slowly but unmistakably moving against the backdrop of the starry sky. Probably, by tomorrow, the only things left here would be the signaler for the dynamic positioning system and the wave dampers.

Nothing major.

For them, it would be easy to rebuild both someday.

Aphrodite sucked in huge quantities of water, spouted them out again, and moved.

He had entered the Control Tower to check the control computer and the reactor, making sure that the motive system was still functional.

Yūichi stood on the top deck of the hydrofoil, leaning against the handrail, watching the slowly receding Aphrodite.

Was he sad?

Or was he, maybe, sending a message of celebration on Aphrodite's new beginning—and to the young people of the new generation, who were going to fight for the dream his own had failed to achieve?

He couldn't say.

He didn't know what he felt.

For now, not thinking anything, he was merely watching Aphrodite receding into the distance.

In spite of which . . .

"When Aphrodite began to move, the captain and crew were surprised as hell." He heard the voice of Crane, the news reporter, from behind him. "They can't decide what to do about it."

". . ." Yūichi didn't turn around.

Crane leaned against the rail next to Yūichi. "What are they planning to do with Aphrodite now?" he asked. "Wherever they go, there will be a big uproar . . . I don't think they'll be welcomed anywhere."

"At any rate, they have time now . . ." said Yūichi, quietly. "And, being who they are, I think they'll think of something."

Crane stared at Yūichi's face from the side, then smiled knowingly. "Why don't you confess? You did it, right?"

"Don't be ridiculous." Yūichi shook his head. "Just like I told the captain before, I stole the submersible and escaped from Aphrodite."

"Yeah, I heard you," said Crane, shaking his head.

"At any rate, I've given up on writing that report about astronauts being unable to adapt to reality. You are certainly not that: you're magnificent! And I thought you had merely come to Aphrodite

2063 :: Age 30

because you were sentimental. I was sure wrong...
When you heard Aphrodite was going to be blown up, you came to save it, right? A knight, you are."

"..." Yūichi kept watching Aphrodite. Silent, he neither affirmed nor denied Crane's words.

After a while, Crane spoke in a strangely low voice. "You really loved Aphrodite."

"Mm..." nodded Yūichi, then seemed to sink into thought for a minute. A smile slowly floated to his lips.

"Yeah, I guess so," he finally said. "I certainly didn't hate it."

▲▲▲▲
Author's note

The author would like to express his appreciation to the following writers for the use of their books in preparing this manuscript:

Kaijō Toshi [Floating Cities], Kikutake Kiyonori. Kashima Shuppankai.

Transportation in the World of the Future, Harold Hellman. M. Evans. Translated into Japanese by Oka Hisamaro as *Mirai no Kōtsū* and published by Kashima Shuppankai.

Kaiyō Kōgaku Nyūmon [Introduction to Oceanic Engineering]. Gōda Shuhei et al., Kōdansha.

▲▲▲▲

About the Author

Yamada Masaki was born in Nagoya, Japan in 1950. He attended Meiji University, graduating with a degree in Economics. His debut novel *Kamigari* won the sixth Seiun Prize (the Japanese equivalent of the Hugo Award) in 1975. Three of his other books have also won Seiun prizes: *Chikyū: Seishin Bunseki Kiroku*, in 1978; *Hōseki Dorobō*, in 1980; and *Kishin Heidan*, in 1995. He is the author of over one hundred forty works in a wide range of styles, including science fiction, adventure, general fiction, police procedural and mystery, and fantasy, often deliberately blurring the lines between genres. While widely known as a science fiction author in Japan, but has been building on this reputation by challenging the mystery world as well with novels like *Sōjō no Tsumikiuta*, awarded eighth place in the Bunshun Best Mysteries of the Year, and *Mystery Opera*, which won the Mystery Writers of Japan Award.

▲▲▲▲
About the Translator

Daniel Jackson is the pseudonym of an American-born professional translator and long-term resident of Japan. He and his family live in a restored and renovated country home, said to be a classic of its type. Floor space not occupied by dogs is home to his large collection of English and Japanese books.

▲▲▲▲

About the Artist

Kobayashi Osamu (小林治) was born in Tokyo in 1964. He is active in a range of illustration, design and video presentation work in various media, including commercials, games and animation, with a twenty-six part animated TV program launching in 2004. He also plans to complete an animated work for distribution through movie theaters in 2005, which he describes as "Heavily into music, boy-meets-girl plot, and probably a musical." Other ongoing projects include work on a number of OAV animations (*Blue Submarine #6*, *Gad Guard*, etc.), several NHK puppet theater shows including *20,000 Leagues Under the Sea*, and games like *Gunglaive* and *Grandia*, as well as TV commercials for firms including Toyota Motor, Symantec, and Canon.

Printed in Great Britain
by Amazon